Leaving Atlanta
Henry Vogel

Published in the United States of America by Henry Vogel.

Cover art: Bill Neville & Chuck Wojtkiewitz

Cover colors: Maja Opacic

Cover design: Getcovers.com

ISBN: 978-1-959859-20-8 (ebook)

ISBN: 978-1-959859-21-5 (paperback)

First publication: June 2025

For David Willis. There would be no Southern Knights without him.

David Shenk – alias Electrode. A self-created superhero, natural leader, and experienced crime fighter, he drove the formation of the Southern Knights. His electricity-based powers give him the ability to fly and shoot electrical bolts from his hands.

Kristin Austin – no alias. Short, super strong, and bulletproof, Kristin's temper has a short fuse. She's more feisty than skilled, but her tenacity offsets her lack of training. She is the heart of the Southern Knights.

Dragon – alias Mark Dagon. He is humanity's myths and legends come to life. Dragon possesses fiery breath, prodigious strength, and the power of flight. Through a magical draconic quirk, he can transform into a normal, non-powered human.

Connie Ronnin – no alias. Connie is a former Olympic silver medalist in fencing with psychic abilities. Her powers manifest through her psychic sword, and are constrained by it. Anyone struck by her blade reacts as if they'd been hit by a real sword. The effects fade away over time.

Aramis Merrow – no alias. He is a young sorcerer who spent over two hundred years in magical suspension. Barely eighteen and far from comfortable in the modern world, Aramis weaves the elemental threads of reality to create mind-bending effects.

CRUSH HOUR

Afternoon rush hour east of downtown Atlanta. Ten lanes of frayed nerves inching down I-85. Six lanes of growing impatience crawling along I-285. Air conditioners spewing lukewarm breezes in futile attempts to cool the four-wheeled ovens covering every inch of the roadway. Within the rolling kitchen appliances, the citizens of Atlanta baked to sweltering perfection under an August sun that blazed through a Southern summer sky of washed-out blue. Engines snarled. Horns blared. Drivers screamed.

And that was *before* these twin currents of roasting road rage collided at the twisting, incomprehensible work of modern art the Georgia Department of Transportation called the Tom Moreland Interchange. Tempers flared and obscenities flew as hapless drivers missed their exits, and common sense evaporated in the face of the cacophony.

But today was different.

The engines were silent. The horns mute.

Eyes that should have remained locked on the next bumper instead squinted into the distance. What they saw astounded their owners and drew them from their vehicles for a better look at the terrifying source of the traffic jam.

Half a mile from the criss-crossing roads, two towering, gleaming, humanoid machines strode down the middle of the interstate. Concrete cracked under their feet, steel buckled beneath their heavy tread, and people fled before them, abandoning their cars seconds before massive feet flattened them.

"What the hell *are* those things?" a man asked, staring at the figures from the middle of an overpass.

"They look like they're from a movie, Dad," his young son replied. "Sorta like little Iron Giants or something."

"Cool!" the boy's little brother said. "D'you think they gots guns and stuff?"

The child-rearing, autocorrect part of their father's brain responded without conscious thought. "Do you think they *have* guns and stuff?" Then he took his sons' hands. "We've got to get off this bridge!"

Dragged along by their father, the boys never took their eyes from the figures and their path of destruction. They spotted the sky-borne figures before anyone else.

"Look, Dad," the older boy pointed, "it's the Southern Knights!"

As the boy spoke, a mini-gun rose smoothly from a mechanical figure's shoulder and swiveled towards the approaching superheroes.

～

"**H**old on, young ones," Dragon rumbled as he tucked his wings and dove for the ground.

Astride the mighty wyrm's back, Aramis, Connie, and Kristin tightened their legs. They squinted into the reflected glare from a thousand cars and studied the scene below them.

"What the hell *are* those things?" Kristin asked.

The petite blonde's com carried her question to her teammates' ears. Electrode's eyes darted from the giant mechanical constructs to the chaos ahead of them, but his agile mind noted Kristin's question.

"Mechs," Electrode replied.

"Gee, thanks, fearless leader," Kristin said. "In English, please?"

"Think walking tanks with a human pilot," Electrode replied. "That's not entirely accurate, but—"

"It's good enough," Kristin interrupted.

Below, people fled before the massive figures. Most abandoned their cars and sprinted for the emergency lane. Brakes squealed and wheels turned hard as drivers avoided terrified commuters who dashed into the narrow space between bumpers. Other drivers panicked, turned their cars away from the approaching metal monstrosities and tried ramming their way through the gridlock. Steel ripped and bent as cars ground into each other. Fists shook. Faces reddened. Mouths gaped in incoherent cries of fear and fury.

"Aramis," Electrode called into his com, "get Connie and Kristin down there now!"

From Dragon's back, the young sorcerer's eyes lost focus as he peered into the magical realm. His silver bangs curled up like tiny horns as a tangled web of multi-colored threads came into focus before him. With the ease of one born to a magical family, Aramis forced order onto the swirling chaos before him as he sought the lines of magical energy he needed.

"Kristin, you're on citizen safety," Electrode continued. He glanced at Aramis. The mage's blank expression told him

Aramis's mind was elsewhere. "Have Aramis shield the bystanders from that mini-gun."

"Got it, boss," Kristin replied.

"Connie," Electrode added, "make for the mech with the mini-gun. I'll distract the pilot's attention. Do you think you can climb to the cockpit?"

The tall brunette examined the mech briefly and replied, "I believe so. It will be easier if it's standing still."

"I'll do what I can," Electrode replied. "Dragon, can you keep the other mech occupied while we deal with his partner?"

"**Indeed**."

"Good," the team leader said. "Knights, go!"

Aramis drew golden threads from Connie and Kristin to him. He wove their golden threads around a thin green thread from a patch of weeds sprouting through the median before the mechs, and imposed his will upon the weave. The three teammates disappeared from Dragon's back and appeared between the mechs and the people of Atlanta.

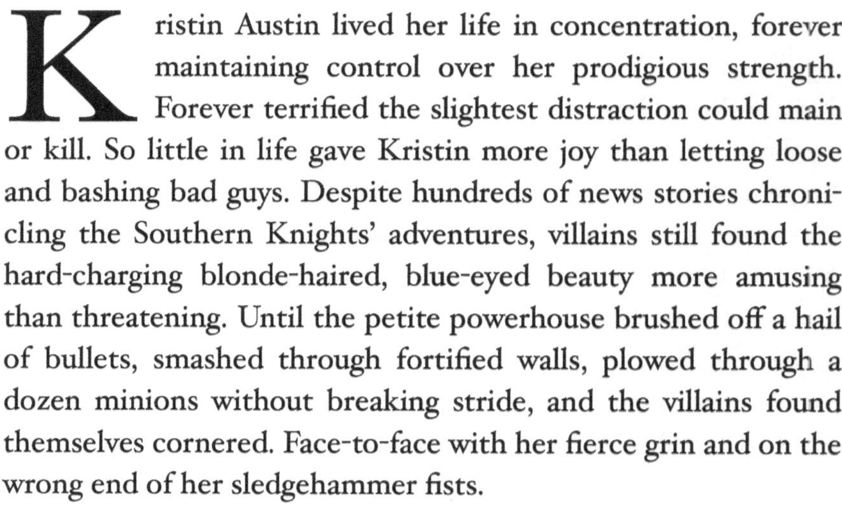

Kristin Austin lived her life in concentration, forever maintaining control over her prodigious strength. Forever terrified the slightest distraction could main or kill. So little in life gave Kristin more joy than letting loose and bashing bad guys. Despite hundreds of news stories chronicling the Southern Knights' adventures, villains still found the hard-charging blonde-haired, blue-eyed beauty more amusing than threatening. Until the petite powerhouse brushed off a hail of bullets, smashed through fortified walls, plowed through a dozen minions without breaking stride, and the villains found themselves cornered. Face-to-face with her fierce grin and on the wrong end of her sledgehammer fists.

But the true mark of a hero is the ability to do what's needed, and to do it to the best of her ability, even if it isn't what she wants to do. Faced with a pair of thirty-foot-tall mechanical men and surrounded by pandemonium and panicked people, Kristin did the hardest thing in the world. She turned her back on the two foes marching her way. She turned her back on her teammates, who stood firm before the mechs. And she charged headlong into the mass of tangled metal that had once been commuters' cars.

High-pitched squeals of terror cut through the din of racing engines, the whir of the massive mechs' servos, and the shouts of people running for their lives. Kristin's eyes darted to the left, spotting a minivan filled with frantic figures inside. A delivery van pressed against the driver's side, an SUV blocked the passenger doors, and a pickup truck had plowed into the rear hatch. Two young girls beat on the backseat windows while their parents kicked in vain at the front windshield.

Kristin bounded onto the nearest trunk and leapt to the minivan's roof. She landed with a thump, which panicked the girls even more.

"Daddy!" one girl wailed. "Get me out! Getmeout getmeout getmeout!"

The kicks to the windshield redoubled in intensity, so no one inside the car heard Kristin shout, "I'm here to help!"

Kristin peeked over the minivan's edge and made sure she was behind the passenger seats, and she slammed her fist through the metal. Grabbing the ragged edges of the hole she'd just made, she peeled the roof back as easily as a normal person peeled back the seal on a peanut butter jar. Tear-streaked faces turned her way as the children stared at her in wide-eyed terror.

"Hi." Kristin kept her voice light and friendly as she reached for the first child. "I'm Kristin. What's your name?"

Connie crouched low and ran towards the mech with the mini-gun. A shadowy figure within the massive armored figure's cockpit turned its head her way. The multi-barreled gun matched the head's movement and opened fire at the same time. Rounds shredded abandoned cars and chewed the pavement as the path of destruction tracked towards her. The lone Knight dove behind a pickup truck's bed, kept low, and hurried to the front fender.

"I need that distraction now, Electrode." Despite the massive firepower turned her way, Connie's voice remained cool.

A glowing form flashed in the corner of Connie's eye as Electrode swooped into the pilot's view. Bright golden beams erupted from his hands. One bolt splashed on the pilot's canopy, blinding the man within. The mini-gun swung wildly as the pilot's head turned towards the closer threat.

"Thanks," Connie said. "There's no cover between me and that thing, so please keep it busy."

A shadow passed over Connie, and a minivan, its roof ripped open like a can of sardines, crashed down between Connie and the mech. A second later, a white delivery van landed between the minivan and the mini-gun.

"Ask, and you shall receive," Kristin said.

A man's outraged voice carried over Kristin's open comm. "Hey, that was my van!"

"And that's my friend," Kristin snapped. "You know, the woman risking her life for you?"

"You leave her alone!" a child's voice cried.

"I've got more cars if you need them," Kristin called, and her voice drowned out the bickering bystanders.

"That should do for now," Connie replied.

Without another word, she dashed from her hiding place behind the pickup truck towards the cover of the minivan.

The second Aramis felt pavement beneath his feet, he released the weave he and his companions had ridden from Dragon's back to the ground. The golden threads that bound Connie and Kristin to him sprang back into the two women as they sprinted off in opposite directions. Aramis focused on the lines of magical energy flowing around him.

Aramis found little to work with in the congested river of concrete and asphalt. Some living, green magical strands waved from weeds poking through the highway. He'd used one to anchor his teleportation spell, but there were far too few to weave into a shield. Without an energizing wind and weighed down by oppressive humidity, the white threads of air hung limp and devoid of the energy he'd need to deflect high velocity rounds. With a grimace, Aramis turned his sorcerer's gaze to the road. The dense, gray weave of asphalt yielded strength, but the pavement was magically dead. Without a massive infusion of energy, he could never manipulate it.

"Dragon," Aramis swept his arm towards the open area Connie had just run through, "animating fire would be most appreciated."

"Very well. Shield your eyes."

Aramis closed his eyes and covered them with both hands, and still the bright light of Dragon's flame penetrated and left an afterimage. But his sorcerer's sight remained unaffected, and Aramis couldn't resist a smile as the bright red strands of magical fire poured energy and temporary life into the dull gray of the highway.

Aramis's mystical fingers took a handful of precious golden

threads from his own body. He ignored the sharp pain and flash of fatigue as he ripped the strands from his body and fed them into the scorched ribbon of concrete before him. His own life-force spread through the concrete and put it under his command. With a grunt of effort, he broke the bonds tying flame-animated gray threads from the rest of the road.

Those who stood watching the Knights battling the mechs gasped as a wall of what had been the I-85 Southbound lanes rose between them and the mechs. They never saw the mini-gun swing their way, nor saw the rounds slam into the now-vertical strip of pavement. Few even noticed the young man who levitated himself over the newly-erected barrier to join the battle beyond it.

~

A twenty-ton being shouldn't notice the absence of a few hundred pounds, but Dragon felt his three friends and teammates vanish, and his flying showed it. No longer concerned with unseating his riders, the massive dragon tucked his wings and followed Electrode's glowing trail as he dove for the ground.

With the sharp eyes of a flying predator, Dragon saw the trio appear far below. He watched Kristin ignore her instinct to charge into the fray and instead rush to help those who couldn't escape the mechs' path of destruction. Connie, whose psychic abilities were as powerful as they were short-ranged, ran towards the mech with the mini-gun. Despite the apparent mismatch between the mech and swordswoman, Dragon trusted Electrode's commands. He angled his descent towards the second mech and considered how best to distract its pilot.

Aramis's request for fire crackled in the comm that Electrode tailored for the world's largest superhero. He spat a long tongue of white hot flame and watched it wash over the pavement below, directing it over the ground between the young sorcerer and the second mech. Pavement writhed in the brutal heat of Dragon's flame. Satisfied with the result, Dragon closed his mouth and saved his remaining flame reserves for later use.

~

A conflagration raged around the second mech for a moment before it died away. Inside the cockpit, the pilot heeded blaring heat alarms and engaged emergency cooling systems. Fans whined and blew scorching wind across the heat sinks installed throughout the mech's superstructure. Thermal waves rose from every vent on the mech, rippling the air around the mech as its internal temperature rapidly dropped. Red warning lights turned amber and then green, as the mech's systems came online again.

The pilot's fingers danced over the controls as Dragon landed right in front of him. He raised the mech's right arm, and an auto-cannon slid free of its housing inside the hand. A savage grin spread across the pilot's face, certain he couldn't miss his scaled enemy at such close range.

Before the pilot could draw a bead on the Knight, Dragon lashed the metal monstrosity with his tail. Caught mid-step, the blow jarred the pilot and the mech staggered sideways. The auto-cannon round whistled off into the distance and exploded against the interchange's retaining wall.

As the pilot cursed his luck, his eyes focused on the crisscrossing overpasses ahead. Cars stretched across every inch of the structures, and people swarmed among them as they abandoned their vehicles and scrambled to get off the elevated roadways. The pilot's grin widened as he deployed his mech's missile battery.

KNIGHT MOVES

Electrode flew an ever-shifting course. He dived and rose. Twisted and turned. Zipped back and forth before the mech. Its shoulder mounted mini-gun spun left and right and up and down as the mech pilot's head tracked Electrode's movement. The Southern Knights' team leader planned his moves as carefully as time allowed, ensuring his path never crossed in front of unprotected bystanders. Mini-gun rounds slammed into the roadway shield Aramis created, ripped through abandoned cars, and shot harmlessly into the sky. But none rent flesh, smashed bones, or ended lives.

The pilot will realize what I'm doing soon, Electrode thought. Aloud, he asked, "Connie, are you in position?"

"Yes," she replied. "I'm behind the delivery van, fifteen feet from that thing's right foot."

Electrode spun in a tight loop and soared over the mech's line of fire. "The pilot has to get to the cockpit somehow. Can you see rungs on the back of the leg?"

"Yes. Do you think they continue up its back?"

"They should." Twin bolts of electricity blazed from Electrode's hands and painted the mini-gun's mount. Insulation charred, but kept the blasts from arcing into its motors. Electrode asked, "Are you ready?"

"Say the word," Connie replied.

Electrode flew straight up and fired at the cockpit. "Go!"

The bolts splashed over the canopy and bright light washed out the pilot's vision. He never saw the lithe swordswoman sprint to his mech's left foot. He didn't wonder how she kept her footing as she raced over the broken pavement and the spent shell casings that littered the ground around his mech. He didn't know she had moved at all, even as she caught the lowest rung and began her long climb.

Electrode saw Connie's dash, marveled that her feet found the few spots clear of debris, and he felt one worry fade into the back of his mind as she scaled the mech's leg.

The mech's waste heat radiated from the metal rungs and scorched Connie's hands. It flowed through the soles of her shoes and roasted her feet. She pushed the pain aside and climbed on. The rungs continued up the mech's back and ended next to a small hatch in the back of its head. But the rungs were designed for a pilot ascending and descending an unmoving mech, not one on the move.

Halfway up, the mech took a violent, twisting step that jarred Connie's feet and her right hand from the ladder. She dangled from her left hand and flailed ten feet off the ground. Sweltering gusts from heat sinks on the mech's back washed over her as she fought to maintain her tenuous hold on the blazing metal. Connie drew on her decades of fencing experience—practicing through injuries, stressful competitions, the distractions of the Olympic Games—and willed her sweat-slick palm to keep its hold on the ladder. But she still nearly lost her grip before the mech's motion paused, and she could swing back towards the ladder. She grabbed the rung with her right hand and braced her feet against the mech's leg. Connie took a second to secure herself, put one foot on the closest rung, and resumed her climb. She reached the top rung seconds later and grabbed the wheel that sealed the mech's entry hatch. It didn't turn.

"Electrode," she called, "the hatch is locked from the inside."

"Damn," he replied. "You might as well—"

"I have another idea," Connie said, her voice as calm as ever. "Just be ready to catch me."

"Catch you? What are you doing?"

Connie ignored the question as she sought handholds on the mech's head. Overlapping plates and equipment bulges served almost as well as the rungs had. She tuned out the mini-gun firing three feet to her right, pressed her body against the mech's metal skull, ignored the blistering heat, pulled herself on top of the mech, and crawled towards the cockpit canopy.

From the corner of his eye, Dragon spotted a panel open in the center of the second mech's chest. He concentrated on the opening and drew breath for another burst of flame. Char grilling the thing's outside had only slowed it down, but a flame strike inside its chest should do more damage.

Through smoke and haze, ignoring panic and pandemonium around him, Dragon saw what slid from within the mech's chest. Missiles. Four rows of missiles. Electrode, with his vast storehouse of scientific and technological knowledge, would probably recognize the make, model, and specifications of the missiles at a glance. Dragon didn't have such knowledge, so he drew upon three thousand years of experience with humanity's weapons of war. He had spent most of those millennia on the receiving end of mankind's weaponized wrath—and realized the missiles' true threat.

Not to him. Nor to his teammates. But to the thousands of people stuck on the maze of overpasses half a mile away.

"Kristin! Aramis!" he called into his comm. **"Car. Trap shoot. *Now!*"**

~

Urgent and commanding, Dragon's voice blared in Kristin's ear. She recognized the simple code phrase from hundreds of hours of practice and acted on instinct. Kristin grabbed the nearest car and spun like a discus thrower, building momentum for a record toss. But no Olympic athlete ever tried throwing such an unbalanced, non-aerodynamic hunk of steel.

"Hey," a bystander shouted, "that's my new car!"

If Kristin heard the complaint, she ignored it as she spun once, twice, and then released the car after a third revolution. It arched up and away from the fight and down the median toward the distant interchange.

Dragon's tongue of flame enveloped the car a hundred feet from Kristin. Metal twisted and boiled under the blast, and drops of molten steel flew off in all directions.

~

Aramis sagged as he tore more threads from his body and poured his own life force into the air around the flying, roiling, molten mass that had once been a car. He wove his golden threads into the white threads of air, awakening them. His fingers twisted and intertwined as Aramis wove the now-living air into a mystical net, then spun it into a wind that caught the white hot droplets and kept them from splattering bystanders.

The mech pilot launched his missiles. With high-pitched whooshes, sixteen fingers of death streaked past the Knights and towards the thousands of people packed on the overpasses ahead. A chorus of tones told the pilot his missiles had locked onto a target. Then he cursed as all sixteen made minor course corrections and slammed into the super-heated target Kristin, Dragon, and Aramis had placed between the missiles and the interchange. Massive explosions sounded as the missiles blew what was left of the car into shards.

With his mystical net already in place, Aramis fed the suddenly abundant energy into his spell. He shredded more of his own life weave as he fought for control of the forces that raged inside the vortex. Energy beyond anything he'd ever controlled battered his wall of wind and threatened to overwhelm it. Aramis gave up on containing the maelstrom, and redirected it instead.

He stretched the vortex into a cone pointing back at the mech, and then opened the tip of the cone. Pent up energy poured through the opening. Aramis's fingers flew, ripped another golden thread from his life force, and he wove a channel in the dead air between the cone's open tip and the mech. Visible only to Aramis's mystical sight, the channel guided the force of the exploding heat-seeking missiles back at their source.

White hot metal and scorching air slammed into the mech, melted its chest plate, and rocked it back on its metal heels. Inside the cockpit, alarm lights flashed as the pilot's hands flew over the controls, fighting to keep the mech on its feet. Just when the pilot thought he had things under control, Dragon hurtled out of the smoke and charged at him.

Awake of light trailed Electrode as he streaked around the first mech. Mini-gun rounds ripped through the sultry air, pocked the crumbling roadway shield raised to protect the bystanders, and tore into abandoned cars. They didn't rip through Electrode's flesh, but the mech pilot's aim was improving.

From the pilot's new firing pattern, Atlanta's first superhero realized the pilot had figured out the limits of Electrode's evasion and changed from reacting to anticipating the hero's moves. The mini-gun fired low just before Electrode's path brought him past Aramis's shield, then high when unshielded bystanders forced Electrode into a climb. Electrode knew he had no room for error. Worse, he knew the pilot only had to get lucky one time.

Through the mini-gun's din, Electrode heard the unmistakable sound of launching missiles. As they whistled overhead, he willfully ignored them. He had teammates dealing with the other mech, and Electrode trusted them to handle the situation. With his concentration divided between evading the mini-gun and watching for Connie, he couldn't risk any distractions. Not even for a quick look at the missiles.

Then Connie's sweat-streaked face appeared above the mech's head, and Electrode gave her all of his attention.

Connie, her hands raw and red from the sizzling metal she clung to, tightened her grip as the pilot reversed his mech's left swivel and rotated it back to the right. She adjusted to the change in motion, blinked away involuntary tears as she fought her instinctive reaction to release her scorching handholds, and pulled herself up to the top of the mech's head.

Connie crawled across the rounded top of the mighty mech. She balanced the need for haste against the knowledge that she'd only have one chance to take out the pilot. The three-second journey across the blazing surface felt like three minutes, but Connie finally caught sight of the cockpit canopy's top edge. She braced her feet, tightened her left hand's grip, and let go with her right hand.

Precariously balanced atop the gyrating mech, Connie willed her psychic powers to life. Dormant neurons fired as her subconscious mind responded. Awakened by her call, Connie's powers roared to life. Energy flowed down her arm, through her throbbing right hand, and formed her ghostly, glowing psychic sword.

Without a second thought, Connie raised her right hand and pushed herself forward. She went over the front edge of the mech's head. Gravity caught her, pulling her towards the rubble-strewn pavement far below. But as Connie slid down the mech's head, she peered inside its cockpit. A slack-jawed, wide-eyed man stared back at her.

Poised for this second, Connie thrust her right arm at the canopy. Her psychic sword passed through it as if it wasn't there. The pilot raised a hand to ward off the attack. The blade stabbed through the hand, which flopped over as Connie's psychic powers temporarily severed the nerves connecting the hand to the pilot's brain. Her sword point drove between the pilot's eyes and pierced his skull. Her psychic powers flowed through the blade and into the man's brain. The psychic surge overloaded the pilot's mind. His mind shut down in self-defense, and the pilot slumped into unconsciousness. The mech immediately mimicked its pilot's motion, grinding to a halt and bowing its head. Connie tumbled off the canopy and plunged toward the ground thirty feet below.

~

As Dragon bore down on the remaining mech, its pilot instinctively extended his arms in defense. Servos whined as the mech mimicked the pilot's movement, and extended its arms, too. Before Dragon crashed into the steel fists swinging his way, he spread his wings and leapt into the air. With one powerful stroke, he rose above mech and grabbed its arms with his front legs. Talons pierced steel and Dragon pulled the arms as he flew so closely over the cockpit that the pilot could discern individual scales on Dragon's chest.

Irrationally afraid the twenty-ton reptile would carry the twenty-five ton mech aloft and then drop it, the pilot fought against Dragon's grip on his mech's arms. The arms didn't pull free from Dragon's talons, but the mechanical muscles matched the reptilian ones. The arms stopped moving. But Dragon kept going, and the mech had to go with him. Already precariously balanced after Aramis channeled explosive energy and the remains of the car at it, Dragon's flight dragged the mech's head and shoulders backwards. The pilot realized his error too late as Dragon released the arms and the mech toppled backwards.

"Small one," Dragon called, a hint of mirth in his growl. **"I have brought the opponent low. Even you can reach it now."**

~

Electrode looped backwards, up and over the mini-gun's constant stream of rounds.

When will this thing run out of ammo? he wondered.

Then Connie slid down the mech's face. Her glowing blade flashed as she stabbed at the cockpit. From the back of Electrode's logical mind came the expectation the sword would hit the canopy and stop there. But he knew the weapon was only a visible representation of Connie's psychic power, and served to focus those powers in the physical world, prescribing the extent of their range from the marvelous mind that wielded the blade. It pierced the canopy as if it wasn't there.

A mechanical arm lifted in self defense, too late to stop Connie's thrust. The hand suddenly swung free, and Electrode guessed the psychic sword sliced through the pilot's hand. Then the shadowy figure inside the cockpit fell forward.

The mini-gun fell silent, its barrel drooping. The mech's head and shoulders slumped and all other motion stopped. Already sliding down the mech's face and with no handholds, Connie dropped from the mech into Electrode's waiting arms.

"You took a colossal risk, Connie," he said. "What if I hadn't caught you?"

"I knew you would," she replied. "And I had to stop that machine gun before the pilot got a lucky hit."

"It's a mini-gun," Electrode responded without thinking.

"It's not shooting anymore," Connie said. "That's all I care about."

Electrode rounded the stationary mech, and both Knights peered through smoke and dust swirling around the second mech. Dragon's wingtips appeared above the debris cloud and swept down again. A second later, his entire body flew into sight. Then the ground shook as the massive mech toppled.

Kristin sprinted to the downed mech. "Nice job, Greenie!"

"Why do you persist with that nickname?"

"Maybe," Kristin said as she pulled herself onto the mech's

chest, "it's because you're green. Why do you call me Small One?"

Dragon spread his wings wide and banked into a tight turn. **"Maybe it's because you are small."**

"*Everyone* is small compared to you!"

"Indeed, but *you* are small compared to everyone."

"Being small has its advantages." Kristin ducked as a blindly swiping arm brushed her back. Kristin jumped from the mech's chest to its head. "But what's so great about being green?"

"Watch for the other hand, Kristin!"

The dim sunlight that penetrated the dust cast a dimmer shadow as the pilot raised its right hand. He facepalmed his mech, hoping to crush Kristin between the hand and the canopy.

Kristin raised both hands over her head and caught the descending hand. The force of the blow drove her to one knee, but she bent no further.

"Thanks for the warning, Dragon," she said, as a fierce grin spread across her face.

She balled her right hand into a fist and punched the canopy. The pilot's eyes widened in shock when the petite blonde held the mech's palm at bay with one arm. Panic replaced shock as the canopy shattered where her small fist struck.

"Trying to squash me wasn't very nice," Kristin said, and hit the canopy a second time.

Her fist punched through and she reached for the pilot. Trapped in his seat by the harness and his control rig, the pilot could only watch as Kristin grabbed his suit and yanked him towards her.

Restraints ripped. Control wires broke. And Kristin smashed the pilot's head into the canopy. She did it again. And again. And kept doing it until his eyes rolled up and his head lolled. Kristin released the pilot, shoved the unresisting hand away from her head, and made a great show of dusting off her hands.

As the smoke cleared, the bystanders saw the Southern Knights busy prying the unconscious pilots from their mechs. The cheers started with those closest to the action but soon rang up and down I-85 and on the overpasses of the Tom Moreland Interchange.

ANALYSIS

The Analyst's eyes darted across a bank of nine screens. Text scrolled, videos streamed, photos appeared and vanished with no apparent rhyme or reason. But the Analyst's eyes rarely stopped moving. His gaze alighted on a video of a street scene, remained still for one second, and then slid to several lines of text scrolling towards the monitor's upper edge. It snapped to a headline for two seconds before it moved on to a celebrity tweet.

To the woman approaching the Analyst, the monitors displayed chaos. A random data dump of anything and everything—the latest news, trending gossip, stock tickers, and anything else that caught the world's attention for a moment. But she knew from experience the Analyst absorbed everything. Filtered it, categorized it, studied it, analyzed it, and produced remarkably accurate future forecasts from the day's events.

She stopped at a line painted on the floor and waited. The ever-changing display drew her eyes. As always, she sought patterns in the data stream. As always, she failed. The information appeared and disappeared faster than her eyes could move.

What little she gleaned faded from her mind as quickly as the data vanished from the screen.

"Yes, Gayle?" the Analyst said.

He didn't turn around. The Analyst *never* took his eyes from the screens during business hours.

"One battle has ended, sir," Gayle replied.

"Two minutes and forty-one seconds faster than I anticipated," the Analyst mused. "The Turkish team lost?"

Gayle licked her lips. In seven years of service, she'd never delivered such contrary news as she brought today. "They are losing, but that's not the battle I meant."

If Gayle's contradiction bothered the Analyst, it didn't show in his posture, movements, or tone of voice. "Which one, then?"

"Atlanta, sir."

"Disappointing," he murmured. "I expected better from the Southern Knights."

"You misunderstand, sir," Gayle said. "The Southern Knights were victorious."

The Analyst stiffened and then did the unthinkable. He spun his chair and looked at Gayle. It took all her willpower to stand her ground before his intense gaze.

"Casualties?" he asked.

"Early reports show significant property damage, but no casualties."

"The pilots?"

"Captured."

The Analyst's eyes widened. Not by much, but the reaction suggested something she never thought possible. Her news *surprised* the Analyst.

"And the mechs?" he asked. "The Southern Knights destroyed them?"

"No, sir. One sustained moderate damage, but they took both of them intact."

"Extraordinary."

The Analyst spun back to his console, tapped a button, and said, "Atlanta. Activate."

Then he did another unexpected thing—he stood up and walked away from his workstation.

"Come with me, Gayle."

She fell into step beside him. "Where are we going, sir?"

"To Mr. Lowe," the Analyst replied. "He may have questions after we deliver this news."

He led Gayle past the consoles where her coworkers sat with their heads bent towards their screens—just two monitors each, for they were mere analysts, not *the* Analyst. The susurration of voices as they dictated their observations merged with the whir of computer cooling fans. The resulting white noise helped ease the tension Gayle recognized in her fellow analysts' set shoulders, taut necks, and grim expressions.

Trained to extract information from chaos, Gayle caught snippets of her coworkers' observations as she and the Analyst swept past.

"...estimate eighteen casualties so far..."

"...bridge collapse at fourteen minute mark..."

"...mech one exploded, pilot dead..."

They emerged from the twin rows of consoles and entered the open space between the workstations and the Door. In her seven years of working for the Analyst, she'd never come this way. No one but the Analyst ever had.

The Analyst looked at Gayle. "This is your first time in No Man's Land, isn't it?"

Surprised by the casual question from the Analyst—another first in an afternoon rapidly filling with firsts—Gayle's tongue tied itself in knots. "No, sir... No, I mean yes. Um, that is—"

The Analyst's mouth stretched into a smile, his eyes lit with amusement, and it transformed him from a supercomputer with a face into a normal human man. An attractive one, even. Gayle felt her face heat from a blush as she offered a timid smile in return.

The Analyst grinned at Gayle, placed his right hand on the biometric reader, and looked into the retinal scanner. Two seconds later, the Door slid open, and they stepped into the elevator beyond. As the Door slid shut, the Analyst put his left hand on another biometric plate and the elevator descended.

Emboldened by the Analyst's behavior in the last minute, Gayle asked, "What's He like, sir?"

The Analyst always had ready answers to the most esoteric questions, yet he paused for several seconds before he said, "Calm. Steady. Unchanging. At least from our point of view. Think of Him as a mountain before the sea of time. Waves expend their lives at the mountain's feet to no apparent effect. The sea alters the mountain, but far too slowly for us to notice. I have read the journals of my predecessors and see a slow progression of His opinions and attitudes, but He's not changed in my fifteen years working directly with him."

"I see, I think," Gayle said. "Is He a dragon, then?"

"No, I've seen the medical evidence. He's human."

"But, how?"

"No one knows, not even Him," the Analyst replied. "The answer to that question is elusive, but it is His second highest priority."

Gayle swallowed the obvious follow-up question as the door slid open and the Analyst led her into the luxurious suite beyond.

A warm baritone said, "This is an unexpected visit, Wes. May I assume the results of one confrontation strayed from your predictions?"

Gayle gave the Analyst a sidelong glance. Intellectually, she knew he must have a name beyond his title. But Wes? It was so...

normal. So human. Then she remembered his grin and wondered what other surprises lurked inside the Analyst's astonishing mind.

"*Stray* is an understatement, sir," the Analyst—no, Wes—said. "Completely and utterly wrong is more accurate."

Mr. Lowe's gaze focused on Gayle, and she couldn't meet its laser intensity. "This is Gayle, the analyst you told me about? The one whose prediction was at odds with yours and those of the rest of the team?"

"It is, sir."

"A prediction she defended in a manner you found...vexing."

"Quite so, sir."

"Since you brought her with you, I surmise events proved her right?"

"They did, sir."

"Gayle," Mr. Lowe said, "the southeastern United States is your assigned territory?" Mr. Lowe waited until Gayle nodded, then continued. "Heroically speaking, your territory encompasses Dallas's Lone Star Rangers, Charlotte's Queen's Guard, and Atlanta's Southern Knights. If memory serves me correctly, you are the only analyst who predicted a Southern Knights victory."

Gayle nodded, "I did, sir."

"You predicted correctly," Mr. Lowe said, "otherwise Wes wouldn't have brought you down here."

She nodded again.

"Why were you right and everyone else wrong?"

She raised her eyes, met and held Mr. Lowe's intense gaze, and replied, "My original conclusion mirrored the others, but... It *felt* wrong, sir, so I changed it."

"Based on a whim? Your feminine intuition?"

"I believe my subconscious mind performed its own analysis, and its conclusions were at odds with the conclusion logic and the data suggested. If that is intuition, then I must answer yes to your question." Gayle drew a deep breath and uttered the heresy she'd never said aloud. "Your people trained me, my colleagues, and the Analyst to ignore our subconscious impulses. I believe the training is wrong, sir, so I rejected it and paid attention when my gut instinct disagreed with the logical conclusion."

"Extraordinary!" Mr. Lowe cried. "I believe Gayle deserves a promotion, don't you, Wes?"

"That is why I brought her with me, sir."

Gayle's focus sharpened. "A promotion?"

"Yes, Gayle," Mr. Lowe replied, "from now on, you work with Wes rather than for him, and report directly to me. Wes will add your biometrics to the system first thing in the morning. Then he'll brief you on the next phase of our operation."

The Analyst's brows drew down. "It's only midafternoon, sir. Why wait until tomorrow morning?"

Mr. Lowe smiled. "Like Gayle, I don't ignore my instincts. And, Wes, my instincts tell me a night on the town will do wonders for both of you."

"You mean like a..." Wes floundered for a moment as if he couldn't remember the correct word, "...a date?"

"Yes, my boy, exactly like a date. With the lovely young woman at your side." Mr. Lowe smiled. "Unless I'm as wrong as your Southern Knights prediction, you'll both enjoy yourselves. Take the Ferrari, spend the night in the penthouse downtown, put every expense on the corporate card, and don't be frugal. May I assume you've initiated the next step in our plan?"

"I have, sir," Wes replied.

Gayle remembered his last action at the console before Wes led her through No Man's Land. What—or who—in Atlanta had he activated?

"Don't worry, Gayle, we'll explain everything tomorrow," Mr. Lowe said, as if he had read her mind. He smiled and made a shooing motion with one hand. "But *tonight* is for fun and relaxation. No work talk allowed, understand?"

Mr. Lowe's lips remained upturned as the pair returned to the elevator. The second the door hid the analysts from view, he took an atomizer from a side table. He gave it a few pumps to build up pressure, sprayed mist throughout the room, and then he took a cautious sniff. With a nod, Mr. Lowe returned the atomizer to its place and strode towards the bathroom. He dropped his clothes into the incinerator, selected the shower's *sanitize* setting, and breathed a sigh of relief as the near-scalding water washed over him.

KNIGHTLY NEWS

Despite the crowd's acclaim, the scene seemed eerily quiet to Kristin. She always felt that way after a major battle, and this had been one of the Southern Knights' biggest. Roaring engines and swirling dust broke the quiet, as the news helicopters jockeyed for landing spots. Kristin heaved a sigh of regret. Talking to the press was her least favorite part of heroing. She just wanted to rest and relax, not spend the next hour parsing dozens of questions for the verbal *gotchas* so many reporters used, in the hopes of standing out from their competitors.

If I look busy, Kristin mused, *maybe they'll leave me alone and talk to Electrode. He's so much smarter than them, they won't trip him up.*

Kristin turned her attention to the mech, whose pilot she had knocked out. She widened the hole in the mech canopy and pulled the pilot from his seat. A soft moan escaped his lips, though his eyes remained shut. She cocked her fist just in case he awoke and needed reminding who was in charge, but the moan slipped into a sigh and faded away. As Kristin carried him to the ground, two Atlanta police officers picked their way through the battle-scarred and debris-strewn median towards her.

"We'll take him off your hands, ma'am," one called.

"On behalf of the APD," the second said, "thank you."

"You guys are the ones who deserve the thanks." Kristin held the pilot as the first officer applied handcuffs. "I'm just glad we got here before these jerks hurt anyone."

"We are, too," the second officer said. He pointed across the outbound lanes of I-85, "My partner and I were on the frontage road over there when these things showed up. We were gearing up to come after them when you Knights got here."

And people call us *brave*, Kristin thought as the officers carried the pilot away. She glanced at the second mech and saw another pair of officers take the second pilot into custody. Satisfied the situation was well in hand, she spotted something out of place in the wreckage surrounding her. A teddy bear, miraculously undamaged, on the ground next to the ripped open minivan. Remembering the terrified young girls she had pulled from the car, Kristin picked up the stuffed toy, dusted it off, scanned the crowd for the family, and set off towards them.

A female reporter, cameraman in tow, appeared in front of Kristin. "This is Tina Horne of News 23 reporting live from the scene of the Southern Knights' latest battle. I'm with the Knights' popular team member, Kristin Austin. Ms. Austin, would you answer a few questions for our viewers?"

Kristin noted Tina Horne's fashionable business suit, perfect hair, and immaculate make-up and compared the reporter's appearance to her own sweat-stained t-shirt, disarrayed hair, and grimy face. Not a look she wanted to broadcast across the country, but it was already too late for that.

The strongest Knight forced her mouth into a smile and held up the teddy bear. "Please wait one moment. I'm returning this to a little girl."

Kristin walked around Tina, but the reporter fell in step beside her. The cameraman hurried ahead and filmed the pair as they approached the crowd.

"Would you answer just one question while we walk?" Tina asked.

Somewhere in the back of Kristin's mind, alarm bells rang. But she was tired and focused on the family twenty yards away. Her Southern manners kicked in without conscious thought, and Kristin said, "Okay."

Tina asked, "Do you think these mechanical monstrosities chose Atlanta because the Southern Knights are based here?"

Kristin stopped and stared open-mouthed at the reporter. "*What?*"

Tina had her back to the camera, so it didn't record the smug satisfaction Kristin saw appear on the reporter's face. Tina's voice remained level and professional as she said, "I asked—"

"I heard what you asked," Kristin snapped as she stalked past Tina.

Tina hurried to Kristin's side. "Then why don't you answer the question?"

Kristin's temper boiled. "You're blaming *us* for this attack?"

"Consider this from the city's point of view," Tina declared. "While the Southern Knights bask in the limelight, the city faces a multi-million dollar repair bill for your little show. Where is Atlanta going to find the money to pay for these damages?"

A fat, middle-aged man burst from the crowd and blocked Kristin's path. The Knight veered around him, but the man side-stepped and blocked her way again. Tina Horne stepped out of the camera frame and motioned for the cameraman to keep filming.

He jabbed a meaty finger at Kristin. "You got a lot to answer for, blondie."

"I don't know what you're talking about." She tried walking around the man, but he blocked her path again. "Please stop—"

"My car!" the man shouted. "You destroyed my brand new car!"

Kristin's brow drew down in confusion. "I did what?"

"Don't give me that innocent act!" the man raged. "You threw my car in the air and blew it up!"

Comprehension dawned on Kristin and shredded her already frayed temper. She pointed to the interchange a quarter of a mile away and snarled, "Would you rather I let those rockets destroy the overpasses? The ones with *thousands of people* on them?"

Uncowed, the man leaned forward and poked her in the chest, "I'd *rather* you hadn't destroyed my brand new car!"

As the finger came in for a second poke, Kristin caught and held it. "Keep your hands to yourself, mister."

He tried pulling his hand free of Kristin's grip. When that failed, he set his feet and put his considerable weight into pulling free. "Follow your own damned advice, girl!"

Kristin flashed a real, though malicious, grin and released the hand. Caught off balance, the rotund man stumbled backwards, flailed his arms to catch his balance, and fell on his ample rear end.

"Ask, and you shall receive," she spat and marched past him.

"She has no idea just how right she is," Tina murmured to her cameraman. "We *did* receive, right?"

"Oh yeah. Loud and clear." The cameraman patted his camera. "And in crystal clear high definition."

Tina nodded acknowledgement and dragged the cameraman in Kristin's wake. "Keep filming. You can edit out anything we don't want."

"Don't I always?" he replied.

"You do," Tina agreed. "That's why we make such a brilliant team, Bob."

Ahead, Kristin went down on one knee and held the teddy bear out to a little girl who had her arms wrapped around her father's leg. The man squatted next to his daughter and murmured what Tina assumed were encouraging words. The girl hesitated a few seconds before she reached out, snatched the stuffed toy, and hugged it.

"Thank you so much," the girl's mother said to Kristin.

Tina couldn't hear Kristin's reply but she knew it was something like *I'm just glad we got here in time* or *No thanks are necessary*. The typical crap the Kristin Austins of the world always said to people like Tina Horne. Simple, boring, heroic platitudes. Nothing words that consumed precious seconds of Tina's airtime but which producers *never* let her cut from her interviews.

But today would be different. The brief phone call she received before the copter landed assured her of that. The belligerent fat guy was an unexpected bonus. As if on cue, he stalked past her and Bob, his flabby face red with...what? Probably anger, but Tina didn't rule out overexertion from the effort of lifting his bulk off the ground.

Tina stopped ten feet from the scene. "Bob, can you pick up their conversation from here?"

Bob kept his camera trained on the unfolding scene and muttered, "Yep."

Fat guy stopped and loomed over the still-kneeling Kristin. The little girl's just-forming shy smile vanished, and she retreated behind her father's legs.

"Hey," the fat man wheezed, "I'm not finished with you."

Kristin looked over her shoulder and growled, "Back. Off."

"Or what?" he snarled. "Are you going to push me down again?"

Kristin rolled her eyes. "That's *one* interpretation of events."

The little girl's father took a step towards the fat man. "What's your problem, mister?"

Fat guy looked at the father and shouted, "She destroyed my new car!"

Kristin popped to her feet, and her shoulder caught the looming man's protruding belly. He staggered back a step and fell on his butt a second time.

Hands on hips, Kristin leaned over the fat man and hissed, "Yes, I destroyed your car. So what? I'd do it again in a heartbeat because it *saved lives*!"

The father's face contorted with anger equal to Kristin's and snarled, "She destroyed my car, too! Ripped the roof off and threw what was left into the middle of that fight. But you don't see me complaining, do you?"

Wind ruffled Tina's hair as Electrode flashed by overhead. Kristin took a step back as Atlanta's first hero landed between her and her antagonist.

"Let me deal with this," he said.

"But he's—"

Electrode kept his voice gentle. "Please walk away, Kristin."

"Fine," she snapped, and stomped towards Tina and Bob.

"Are you all right, sir?" Electrode asked as he extended a hand and helped the fat man to his feet.

"She destroyed my car!" he repeated.

"Sometimes these things happen in emergency situations, sir," Electrode said. "But we're insured against..."

Tina tuned out Electrode's calming words as the Southern Knights' petite powerhouse approached. She whispered, "Stay on her, Bob."

"Way ahead of you, Tina," he replied.

Fury burned in Kristin's eyes and her lips moved as she ranted to herself, "Saved their lives. But are they grateful? Hell no! *You broke my stuff*, they whine. Do they think where they'd be if we weren't here? Huh? Nope. *That* never occurs to them. Nuh uh. Not once. But if we *weren't* here? Oh, we'd never hear the end of it!" Kristin punched her fist through the trunk of an already-mangled car. "Maybe we should just pack up and leave. Where would they be then, huh? Yeah, I bet tons of other cities would *beg* us to move there!"

Bob tracked Kristin as she stalked away. Tina watched with growing elation as she mentally constructed the story she'd submit to the station.

"Tell me you got everything," she said.

"Every move. Every expression. Every word." Bob lowered his camera and grinned. "Everything."

Beer in hand, Kristin entered the Hampton House's living room. She ignored the splendid view of the grounds outside the bay window, settled onto the couch, and put her bottle on a coaster on the end table. Connie followed her friend and sat in the chair next to the table.

"Are you okay?" Connie asked.

Kristin took a long pull on the beer, picked up the TV remote, and said, "Yeah. I just wish we could finish *one* fight without some jerk going off on us."

"I understand. That's why I stay in the background during the aftermath."

Kristin shook her head. "You stay in the background because you're an introvert."

Connie sniffed. "I prefer the term *gregarially challenged.*"

"*Gregarially* isn't even a word!" Kristin said.

"Is its meaning clear?" Connie asked.

"You got me there," Kristin laughed. She thumbed the

remote, and the TV came to life. "Shall we see what the news is saying about us?"

"If we must."

"We must. I'm curious what Tina Horne will say. Did you notice how quickly she arrived on the scene?"

"Yes, but I assumed she was the closest reporter when the fight ended."

"Never assume anything when it comes to her." Kristin switched to channel twenty-three. "I asked some other reporters. According to them, Horne's pilot landed minutes before the police gave the all clear."

"That might not mean much," Connie mused. "Once those mechanical things went down, it was obvious they weren't getting up again."

"Obvious to us, maybe. But to someone a thousand feet in the air? I don't buy it."

"What are you implying, Kristin?"

"I don't know," Kristin admitted. "Maybe I'm still pissed off at her for suggesting the attack was our fault."

On the screen, a distinguished news anchor looked into the camera and said, "We switch now to reporter Tina Horne with her exclusive report on the Southern Knights battle at the Tom Moreland Interchange. Tina?"

Tina Horne's face filled the screen. "Thank you, Roger. Today, the Southern Knights faced one of their most difficult battles with the lives of thousands hanging in the balance."

The screen shifted to aerial footage of the fight as Horne provided a concise and accurate description of the action. When the second mech fell, the image switched back to Horne. "City officials thanked the Southern Knights for, and I quote, *their staunch and unyielding defense of Atlanta and its citizens. Our city is lucky to have them.*"

The camera pulled back and a publicity photo of the Knights

appeared next to Horne's head. "Heady praise. But praise I must question."

Kristin rolled her eyes. "There's a shocker."

Horne folded her hands on her news desk, leaned forward, and gazed into the camera. "Is Atlanta lucky to have the Southern Knights? Or..."

A video image of Kristin, grimy with dust and sweat. From off camera, Tina Horne asked, "Do you think these mechanical monstrosities chose Atlanta because the Southern Knights are based here?"

In the video, Kristin's eyes widened. She opened her mouth, and the image froze there. "Ms. Austin did not answer my question. But an answer proved unnecessary."

Horne held up a sheaf of papers. "Atlanta was not the only city attacked in this manner today. Charlotte. New York. Dallas. Los Angeles. Tokyo. Ankara. London."

Each time Horne named a city, a new image of devastation displayed on the screen. She tossed the papers aside and stared into the screen. "And a dozen other cities beyond those. *All* suffered similar attacks. *All* drew the attention of a local superhero team. *All* resulted in hundreds, even thousands of casualties."

"Hey, *we* didn't have any casualties!" Kristin spluttered.

"Property damage in the *billions*."

"Not our fault!" Kristin shouted at the screen.

"And that damage wasn't limited to public property," Horne added.

The angry fat man from the afternoon filled the screen. "She destroyed my new car!"

The father whose family Kristin pulled from their minivan appeared next and shouted, "She destroyed my car, too! Ripped the roof off and threw what was left into the middle of that fight."

Kristin snorted, "Way to take the man's quote out of context, Tina!"

Tina Horne radiated outrage as her face filled the screen. "How many other citizens have suffered grievous physical or financial injuries simply because the Southern Knights chose Atlanta as their home? How many lives have the Knights ruined while *protecting* our city? Think back, viewers. Was life in Atlanta so horrible, so crime-ridden, before the Southern Knights arrived on the scene? Was life in Atlanta so bad that you wouldn't happily return to those days if you could?"

With visible effort, Horne composed herself and addressed the camera. "Does Atlanta need the Southern Knights? I say no. I say the Southern Knights should leave Atlanta and take the dangerous elements they attract with them. But I'm not the only one who holds that opinion."

Kristin's enraged face replaced Horne's. "Maybe we should just pack up and leave. Where would they be then, huh? Yeah, I bet tons of other cities would *beg* us to move there!"

A closeup of Tina Horne's vehement expression filled the screen. "For once, I agree wholeheartedly with a member of the Southern Knights. Yes, Kristin, you *should* pack up. Yes, you *should* leave. Atlanta does not need you. It never did." The camera pulled back as the reporter flashed a tight smile. "I'm Tina Horne reporting for Channel 23 News."

David and Mark hurried into the living room, drawn by Kristin's inarticulate shout. A haggard Aramis dashed out of his upstairs room and peered down at the scene from the top of the stairs.

"I can't—!" Kristin spluttered. "That bitch! Who does she—? Aaaarrrrgggghhh!"

David made placating motions with his hands. "Calm down, Kristin."

"Calm down?" Kristin shouted. "Calm down! Did you—? I mean, seriously! Who in—?"

Aramis gripped the banister and stumbled down the stairs. In a quiet voice, he asked, "What is the matter, Kristin?"

Aramis's words cut through Kristin's fury where David's had not. Concern replaced anger as she turned his way, "Oh no, I didn't mean to wake you up, kiddo. Working magic took a lot out of you today. Go back to bed. I can tell you about it in the morning."

"I appreciate your concern," he replied, "but could you sleep if I had voiced outrage such as you did?"

"No," she sighed and picked up the TV remote. "You might as well sit down while I rewind the broadcast."

The team watched in silence as Kristin replayed Horne's report. Connie, having seen it once, watched her friends instead of the screen.

Over his three thousand years of life, Mark mastered impassivity. He maintained a steady countenance throughout the broadcast. But Connie had an introvert's eye for facial expressions. She caught the slight narrowing of his eyes.

She thought, *Mark will never admit it, but he's angry*.

Growing up as the smartest kid in school, dealing with classmates' cruel taunts taught David how to mask his emotions. It proved a valuable leadership skill when dealing with the Southern Knights' disparate personalities. Connie saw him grimace as Horne relayed the news of the other attacks. David lowered his head for a second. When he raised it again, his expression projected calm once again.

David's concerned.

Exhaustion and youth made Aramis easy to read. His brows drew down, and he tilted his head to the right, all the while stifling a yawn.

Aramis is frightened, Connie realized. *Does this report remind him of the witch hunt that led to his parents' deaths?*

Kristin still radiated anger, and Connie knew it came from the injustice of Tina Horne's allegations. *She's open and straightforward about everything. Even though she's been in the spotlight for years, Kristin still expects everyone else to act the same way she does.*

The replayed broadcast ended, and Kristin said, "See what I mean? It's all innuendo and comments taken out of context."

"Not entirely," David replied. "As much as I hate agreeing with her, it looks as if those two mechs attacked Atlanta to draw us out."

"That doesn't make it our fault," Kristin fumed. "And you can be damned sure she'd be the first and loudest one screaming if we ignored those things!"

"Will we be chased from our home?" Aramis asked.

Kristin hugged him. "No, of course not."

"Kristin is right," Mark said. "Ms. Horne's story will get its moment in the sun, but saner heads will prevail eventually. As long as Ms. Horne is the only person pushing the story, I think it will fade into irrelevance. We just have to wait it out."

INTUITION

As with everything Wes did, he gave driving the Ferrari all of his attention. Gayle marveled when his lips stretched in an unconscious smile, as he ran up through the gears and blew past the speed limit for the winding mountain road. The man beside her in the car was so at odds with the man she knew as the Analyst. At work, he was as close to a robot as someone could be.

Logical.

Analytical.

Knowledgable.

Emotionless.

Distant.

But since she accompanied him to see Mr. Lowe, he'd transformed. Become a human being. One with a quirky sense of humor and charmingly chivalric behavior. He had opened the car's door for her when they left, and again after they reached the finest restaurant in downtown Denver. Wes took the lead in all the ways she believed a man should lead. But when they entered Mr. Lowe's penthouse apartment, he quietly turned the lead over to her.

She requested a drink, which he mixed to perfection. Then Gayle guided him to a loveseat, leaned against him, and sipped her cocktail. They spoke of their lives before they came to work for Mr. Lowe. Revealed starry-eyed teenage dreams. Fell into an intimate silence that neither of them felt the need to break.

Eventually, Wes asked, "There are four bedrooms. Which one do you want?"

Gayle raised her head, looked him in the eyes, and offered a seductive smile. "Yours."

He raised his eyebrows. "And where will I sleep?"

She kissed him softly on the lips. Without speaking, Gayle rose, took Wes by the hand, and led him to the largest bedroom. They slowly undressed each other and tumbled into bed. Then... Soft moans. Gentle caresses. Delighted gasps. Rhythm. Release. And a sense of contentment like she'd never felt before.

Gayle rested her head on Wes's shoulder and let her hand roam over his chest. His breath came slowly and steadily. The deep breathing of sleep.

But sleep eluded Gayle. Not because of the man sleeping next to her. Not entirely because of him, anyway. She had *liked* the Analyst. She would *love* Wes. Her analysis of their work environment had missed that. But, she realized, her intuition had not. It had guided her decisions after dinner, and it hadn't led her astray. Just as it hadn't led her astray with the Southern Knights prediction.

During her seven years working for Mr. Lowe, she analyzed countless disaster scenarios. From swiftly distributing aid to those most affected by a disaster to the best post-disaster investment opportunities. And she analyzed hundreds of theoretical situations. Those ranged from the economic effects of a crop failure on a particular region to the effects of a major apocalypse, such as a massive earthquake that dropped California into the Pacific Ocean.

Gayle loved the theoretical scenarios more than any other part of her job. The research. The mind-freeing flights of fancy. Using the research to rein in the fancies and wrangling it all into a coherent report for the Analyst. Then defending her conclusions against his incisive questioning.

When the Analyst gave them the superhero scenario, she assumed it was just another theoretical exercise. Far more specific than previous exercises, since this one involved such a small number of test subjects. Just the members of the superhero team and the two mech pilots. Though the scenario included thousands of innocent bystanders, she found she could treat them as a single, amorphous organism. Because of the restricted parameters, Gayle finally gave in to her inclination and relied more on intuition than logic. And events proved she'd been right to do so.

That was the real surprise. Not that she'd predicted correctly. But that she saw her conclusions come to fruition through actual events. She had believed the exercise was firmly rooted in the theoretical realm. No danger. No damages. No casualties. Until the reality of the morning.

She marveled at how greatly she had underestimated Mr. Lowe's organization. At the scope of what he had built in his twenty-two hundred years of life. The wealth and technical expertise required to construct three dozen mechs was beyond the capabilities of all but the richest and most powerful nations in the world. Yet Mr. Lowe's organization not only built them, it blithely sacrificed most of them in a single afternoon. Just to gather data on eighteen superhero teams.

On the surface, it made no sense.

But she knew it made perfect sense to Mr. Lowe.

After she applied analysis and intuition, she would understand why it made sense to Mr. Lowe. If stymied, she could probably even convince Wes to help her with the analysis. If she presented the problem to him in terms of serving Mr. Lowe to the best of their ability...

Yes, that would work.

Of course, she'd have to figure out how to get rid of Mr. Lowe by herself. Wes would never turn on him. Not even for her. But she felt certain she could handle that detail on her own.

She vented a soft sigh of contentment, snuggled closer to Wes, and smiled. She was glad she had decided to fall in love with him. Because a woman *should* love the man who would rule the world at her side.

PITCH PARADE

The Southern Knights slept late, something they commonly did after an exhausting fight. But the aroma of coffee, pancakes, bacon, and eggs wafting through the Hampton House roused them. When Kristin entered the kitchen, she found groundskeeper Bryan Daniels busily pouring pancake batter onto a griddle.

Bryan looked over his shoulder. "The first batch is on the table, Kristin. Dig in!"

Kristin yawned and turned towards the coffee maker. "Coffee first."

"Already poured, and the pot is on the table when you want more."

Kristin dropped into a chair at the table, folded her hands, and turned her eyes heavenward. "Thank you, God, for this fine breakfast."

"No disrespect meant to God," Bryan said, "but He didn't cook breakfast."

"True." Kristin sipped her coffee and sighed with pleasure. "He put you on this Earth to do it for Him."

Connie entered the kitchen, with David, Mark, and Aramis right behind her. She took the chair next to Kristin and asked, "Are you suggesting Bryan's only purpose in life is cooking breakfast for us?"

"Of course not," Kristin replied. "He should also cook lunch and dinner." A loud *ding dong* sounded from the front foyer. As Kristin poured syrup over an enormous stack of pancakes, she added, "He should also answer the door."

Bryan headed towards the foyer. "You saved the city yesterday. I'll humor you. Don't let this batch of pancakes burn."

The Southern Knights dug into breakfast and ignored the sound of Bryan opening the front door. If they had paid attention, they'd have heard an indistinct conversation, followed by the sound of the door closing. If they'd looked up from their plates, they'd have seen a bemused Bryan wander back into the kitchen.

"Who was at the door?" Kristin asked around a mouthful of pancakes.

"Um..." Bryan scratched his head. "Mickey Mouse. He's, uh, waiting in the living room. With some others."

Aramis wiped his mouth. "There's a mouse in the house? My mother taught me a simple spell to rid a home of vermin." He raised his hands to prepare for spell casting. "Shall I cast it now?"

Connie reached across and pushed the young sorcerer's hands down. "Mickey isn't that kind of mouse."

"I do not understand," Aramis said. "Also, why do you name your vermin?"

David stood. "We'll explain that a little later. Right now, I guess we should go see what Mickey wants."

The other four Knights and Bryan trailed David into the living room. They found Mickey Mouse and five men in expensive suits waiting for them. Mickey held a sign that read FIGHT CRIME IN THE MOST MAGICAL PLACE ON EARTH.

Aramis nodded in understanding when he saw the mouse costume. "Oh, the mouse is a clown! But aren't the other men too old and fat for circus performers?"

"They're probably just a different, more annoying type of clown," Kristin murmured.

"Kristin," Connie hissed, "remember how little Aramis knows of our time. Please don't confuse him."

Everyone stopped except David, who strode forward and shook hands with everyone, even Mickey. After quiet introductions, David asked, "What brings you gentlemen and gentlemice here?"

"We apologize for arriving unannounced," one man said, and Mickey nodded. "But we wanted to present our offer before anyone else."

David shook his head. "I'm afraid you've lost me. What offer? And what others?"

"The other cities, of course. And rest assured, none of their offers will match ours! Imagine patrolling the skies of Orlando, where it's neither too hot during the day, nor too cold at night. With a headquarters built to your specifications, on sprawling grounds, and conveniently close to all the entertainment Orlando has to offer." The man clapped Mickey on the shoulder. "We'll throw in lifetime passes to *all* Disney parks, memberships in all the best golf clubs, and—."

A second man interrupted, "My... colleague failed to mention lifetime *VIP* passes to all Universal parks, as well."

Irritated, the first man snapped, "Yes, yes, that too. And the Disney passes will also be VIP. I just didn't see any point in mentioning that during the pitch."

"Or *our* passes at all," the second man growled.

The doorbell rang again, and Bryan tore himself away from one of the strangest scene he'd witnessed since the Southern Knights moved into the Hampton House.

David spread his hands. "I'm still lost. What are you asking us to do?"

"Move to Orlando, of course," the first man said.

"Now that you're leaving Atlanta," the second man added.

Kristin cried, "Now that we're *what*?"

"Leaving Atlanta," the first man said.

The second man held up a copy of the Atlanta Journal-Constitution. "Like it says here."

The five Knights turned their attention to the newspaper. Kristin's dirty, sweat-streaked face glared out at them. Above the photo, the headline read KNIGHTS LEAVING ATLANTA?

Footsteps approached from the foyer, and Bryan showed another group of suited men and women into the living room. The woman leading them cast a withering glance at the Orlando team and approached David.

"Why would you want to live and work in a children's playground, when you can come do the same thing in high-tech heaven?" She took and pumped David's hand. "We represent the Research Triangle Park and the cities of Raleigh, Durham, and Chapel Hill. A man of your intellect and education will surely see the advantages of fighting crime with the full support of major technological and biological companies, not to mention the support of three major research universities."

David glanced at his friends, surprise and confusion reflected in his eyes. "Uh..."

The doorbell rang a third time. A moment later, Bryan escorted another group of sharply dressed men and women into the room. As the three groups glared at each other, Kristin asked, "Who do they represent? Dollywood?"

"You're closer than you might think," Bryan muttered.

A man in the finest Italian suit Kristin had ever seen—and she'd seen many of them—flashed a blindingly white smile. "We represent the city of Las Vegas, Miss Austin."

And then the doorbell rang again.

Ading sounded when the express elevator to the Operations Center arrived. Wes released Gayle's hand as the doors parted, and they entered the elevator. "We must maintain a professional demeanor while we're at work."

"I see." Gayle waited until the express elevator doors closed, then leaned against Wes and gave him a gentle, loving kiss. Wes raised his right eyebrow in question, and Gayle flashed a self-satisfied smirk. "We're not at work yet."

Wes couldn't stop the corners of his lips from turning up. "I suppose that's true." The elevator slowed, stopped, and the door opened into the Operations Center. In a low voice, he said, "But now we are."

Gayle wiped the smirk from her face. "I suppose that's true."

Together, the pair walked past the guard station and into Ops. Their strides matched. Their heels clicked on the floor in unison. Thirty-five analysts spun in their chairs and said, "Good morning, Analyst."

The Analyst always gave an acknowledging nod to the analysts before he took a seat at his workstation. This morning, he broke his fifteen year pattern and stopped before the analysts. "Yesterday afternoon, you watched me take Gayle to meet Mr. Lowe."

It wasn't a question, but thirty-five heads nodded.

"You also know that events confirmed the accuracy of Gayle's Southern Knights prediction, illogical as it appeared to the rest of us."

The analysts nodded again.

"In recognition of her exemplary service as an analyst, and

especially in recognition of the courage she displayed by submitting a prediction based primarily on intuition, Mr. Lowe promoted her to a supervisory role, working as an equal alongside me. Her new title is Intuition."

As the Analyst and Intuition turned away, an analyst muttered, "Why does *she* get the promotion? *I* thought the Southern Knights would win, too." Despite her low tone of voice, the comment carried to all ears. From the look on the analyst's face, she hadn't even meant to voice her complaint aloud.

The Analyst turned to face the analysts again. His gaze locked on the woman who voiced the comment. "Stand, Melissa."

With visible reluctance, an attractive woman in her early thirties with dark hair stood. She kept her eyes downcast. "Yes, Analyst?"

"One analyst predicted a Southern Knights victory. Did you submit that prediction?"

"No, Analyst."

"Yet you claim, after the fact, that you also thought the Southern Knights would emerge victorious?"

"I do, Analyst."

"I can draw one of two logical conclusions from your claim." The Analyst held up his right index finger. "You are lying." His right middle finger rose next to the index finger. "You lacked the courage of your own convictions." He lowered his hand. "Which is it, Melissa?"

"I..." Melissa's voice trailed off, and she hunched her shoulders in obvious dismay.

"Analyst," Intuition said, "there is a third conclusion."

The Analyst fought to maintain his impassive expression. He succeeded, but his voice held the barest tinge of incredulity when he asked, "There is?"

"Melissa based her decision solely on logic. As her *training taught her* to do."

"*You* exceeded your training, Intuition."

"I did. But it took me seven years and this specific scenario before I found the courage to do so." Intuition smiled at Melissa. "Melissa, you joined us as an analyst five years ago?"

Hope dawned in Melissa's eyes. "Yes, Intuition."

"Then I'd say you're somewhat ahead of my pace." Intuition glanced at the Analyst. "Would you agree, Analyst?"

The Analyst considered the question and surprised all thirty-five analysts by nodding at Intuition. "If the third conclusion is in play, Intuition, then it could be valid."

Intuition smiled at the Analyst. "I believe Melissa will benefit greatly from my new training program."

Emboldened by Intuition's unexpected support, Melissa asked, "New training program?"

"Intuition training, though I haven't worked out the course details yet." Intuition's smile broadened. "My intuition tells me you'll be an apt pupil, Melissa."

Melissa's posture straightened, and she returned Intuition's smile. "Thank you, Intuition."

"That's all for now," the Analyst said. As he and Intuition turned away from the analysts, she took his hand in hers. Unwilling to make a scene by yanking his hand free, the Analyst hissed, "I told you to maintain a professional demeanor at work!"

Intuition smiled up at the Analyst. "That's Analyst thinking. Intuition believes this is an important step for employee loyalty."

"I don't understand."

"This humanizes you."

"That's not logical. I am human."

Intuition shook her head. "To the analysts, you're an emotionless organic computer. People, no matter how thoroughly trained, do not give their loyalty to a machine. Nor do they give it to an unseen boss like Mr. Lowe."

The Analyst's brows drew down as he considered her words. "But holding hands with you will make them loyal?"

"It's a start." Intuition leaned her head against the Analyst's arm, further emphasizing the intimacy. "And isn't this more fun than pretending we're a pair of sexless robots at the office?"

The Analyst squeezed Intuition's hand. His response told her everything she needed to know. Give her a week, and she'd have the analysts ready to die for the Analyst and herself. Which was necessary, because her plans required sacrifices.

The man in charge of the delegation from Las Vegas, who Kristin had dubbed Flashy Suit Guy, grinned at Aramis. "It's *Vegas*, baby! A good looking guy like you will *love* it there." He leaned closer to the youngest Knight. "You'll find some of our working girls quite accommodating, if you know what I mean."

Obviously uneasy around the man, Aramis tried stepping back. But the forty-odd people packed into the Hampton House's living room hemmed him in. "No, I do not know what you mean."

Flashy Suit Guy wrapped his arm around Aramis's shoulders. "Don't you worry, son. I'll find you a girl who can teach you the ropes."

Aramis cast a pleading look at Kristin, who ignored comments from three other delegations and shoved her way between Aramis and Flashy Suit Guy, who kept his arm draped over Aramis's shoulders. She glared into the Vegas rep's pearly white grin. "Remove your arm."

"I'm just being friendly, Kristin." The man's arm didn't move.

"That's *Miss Austin* to you." She turned her gaze on the rep's arm. "Either *you* remove your arm or *I* will." She offered her best Southern *bless your heart* smile. "And then I'll throw it into the front yard for the dogs to gnaw."

Flashy Suit Guy's grin faltered. "Um, you realize I'm still attached to that arm?"

"You won't be when I'm done with it."

The Vegas rep hastily withdrew his arm and made a show of checking his expensive watch. "My, look at the time! I'm afraid we must be going."

Kristin took Aramis by the arm and plowed a way through the crowd and into the kitchen. She was unsurprised to find Connie sitting at the table, staring out the window with unfocused eyes. "Hey, Connie?"

Connie started and whipped her head around towards Kristin. "Oh! I didn't hear you enter."

"Don't sweat it." Kristin guided Aramis into a chair at the table. "Aramis is feeling, how did you put it last night? Ah, yes, gregarially challenged. He's feeling that."

Connie smiled at Aramis. "Don't worry, we're safe from the crowd in here."

"But those people have already pushed the bounds of propriety by arriving unannounced," Aramis said. "What if they strain those bounds further and invade the kitchen?"

Kristin gave Aramis a sisterly pat on the shoulder. "Then Connie will cut them down with her psychic sword. Unless your mother taught you a spell to get rid of unwanted company?"

Aramis shook his head. "Mother taught me to avoid magic when a boot to the backside would achieve the same result."

"I'm only wearing sneakers, but I'll bet they'll work as well as boots. Especially when you remember no one kicks harder than me!" Kristin headed back towards the living room. "Now, it's time to kick ass and forget names."

~

Promptly at six o'clock, the five Southern Knights and Bryan Daniels gathered around the television for the Channel Twenty-Three news. As before, Connie watched her friends rather than the screen. Despite their silence, she read the expressions easily.

Kristin is still angry about yesterday's news coverage, Connie observed, *and she's steeling herself for more of the same.*

Connie's eyes flicked to David. *David remains concerned, but he believes he's mentally prepared for whatever will come next.*

Her eyes turn to Mark, who appeared relaxed. *Mark still believes the issue will blow over in the long run. But he's three thousand years old, and his idea of the long view could be decades. Maybe centuries.*

Sitting next to David, Aramis almost vibrated with tension. *Aramis is still frightened. He's lost his family and the world into which he was born. Losing the house he grew up in might be one loss too much for him.*

Bryan Daniels hovered behind the sofa, as if unwilling to insert himself among the superheroes. *Bryan grouses about the damage our superheroics do to his landscape, and he puts up an offended front when Kristin adds more Clemson paraphernalia to the house and yard. But he's grown close to us, and hates seeing us on edge like this.*

And what about me? How do I feel? Connie turned her gaze inward. *That's easy. Before I joined the Knights, I pushed people away. For no one could hurt me again if I kept my heart shut tight. And everyone let me get away with it. Until Kristin. Kind, stubborn, loving, never-take-no-for-an-answer Kristin smashed through my defenses and made herself my best friend. And once she opened my heart, she held it open so the David, Mark, Aramis, and Bryan could join her.* Connie ducked her head and wiped her suddenly damp eyes. *What hurts them hurts me. And that is something I will always fight to prevent.*

A television advertisement ended, and the local news anchor appeared. "Once again, our top story tonight centers on the Southern Knights. News Twenty-Three's own Tina Horne is on top of the story."

"I just bet she is," Kristin sniped.

The camera panned to Tina Horne, who sat primly before a blue background. "Good evening, Atlanta. I'm Tina Horne." A photo of the Hampton House filled the screen behind her. Limousines and luxury SUVs packed the driveway and both sides of the road in front of the house. "A circus came to town today, and it destroyed the peace and tranquility of this venerable Buckhead neighborhood."

A video of the scene replaced the still image. Neighborhood traffic edged carefully between vehicles parked along the road outside the Hampton House. Most of the parked cars remained partially on the road, which constricted the two-lane street to a single lane. The camera panned right to left, showing cars backed up in both directions. The parked cars also blocked the sidewalk on both sides of the road, forcing pedestrians to either turn around or walk in the road.

The video shifted to a woman in her mid-thirties, holding hands with two young children. "I just wanted to take my kids to the park to play. But I'd have to walk on the road to get past all these cars." The mother looked over her shoulder at the congested traffic. "No responsible parent would risk her children like that."

The video shifted to a man sitting in his car, stuck in the slow-moving traffic. "What's with all these limos and SUVs? Did someone die or something?"

From off screen, Tina said, "Cities all across the country sent delegations to woo the Southern Knights. These vehicles brought the delegations from Hartsfield-Jackson Airport."

The man let his gaze wander down the line of parked vehicles. "Geez. I wish they'd just hurry up and leave already."

The television image returned to the news studio. Tina Horne shook her head in obvious disgust. "I heard those same words from everyone—driver or pedestrian—I spoke with outside the Hampton House. These citizens tire of the Southern Knights' cavalier attitude towards their neighbors and, in the words of the gentleman who just spoke, wished the Southern Knights would just hurry up and leave."

Kristin threw her arms up. "They were talking about the *cars*, you twit, not us!"

Tina continued, "But one man who has dealt directly with the Southern Knights had more to say. Much more."

An older, overweight man's face filled the screen. A mild breeze ruffled his massive comb over, exposing the man's balding pate, and rheumy eyes stared into the camera.

"Jonathan Barl? And here I thought this story couldn't get any worse." Kristin looked towards the ceiling and spread her arms wide. "Why, God? What sin did we commit to deserve Horne *and* Barl?"

Connie put a hand on Kristin's shoulder. "Let's hear what he has to say."

"I can already tell you," Kristin said. "He'll rant a lot, but it'll come down to 'Southern Knights—menace or threat?'"

On screen, Barl said, "...these so-called superheroes are a menace to the social order, and a threat to our peaceful way of life."

"See?" Kristin cried. "What did I—"

Connie pressed her finger against Kristin's lips. "Shush. We need to listen."

On the television, Barl said, "All Atlantans opened their arms wide in welcome when the Southern Knights first formed. I, more than most. For I also opened my wallet for them, offering financial support for their efforts combating evil in its myriad forms and upholding good old fashioned American decency." Barl grimaced. "And how did these supposed heroes thank me for my generosity? They invited themselves to a social event I hosted, ran roughshod over the grounds, overturned refreshment tables, and even dropped me into my swimming pool!" Barl's face reddened. "Me, a pillar of society and their willing benefactor." Barl glared into the camera. "The Southern Knights showed no loyalty to me then. So I am unsurprised they show no loyalty to our beloved city today. If they want to leave, I say goodbye and good riddance!"

Barl faded out, replaced by Tina Horne's stern face. "The Southern Knights offered no rebuttal to Mr. Barl's accusations."

"Because you didn't ask us for one," Kristin snapped.

"But are any of us surprised that the Southern Knights rub shoulders with the elite from cities across the United States while Atlanta suffers? While Atlantans wonder what will become of them without the Southern Knights' protection, the Southern Knights host an auction for their services. While Atlanta reels under the financial burden of more Southern Knights-driven destruction, the Southern Knights host a circus the likes of which is usually reserved for professional sports teams. While Atlantans piece their lives back together, the Southern Knights seek rich deals from cities desperate for the prestige superheroic teams bring."

The camera pulled away from Tina. "Yes, the Southern Knights hosted a circus today. But what role did they play? Were the Southern Knights the ringmaster, in total control and looking for a big payday? Or were they clowns, with no understanding of the debt they owe to Atlanta? Either way, I and others are more than ready to see the last of them. Leave, Southern Knights. Atlanta does not need you. It never did."

INTUITIVE ANALYSIS

Intuition spent her first day in her new position receiving briefings from the Analyst. Quiet discussions during which he revealed the extent of Mr. Lowe's holdings, operations, and certain plans already in motion. But he steered clear of the situation in Atlanta and deflected her questions. "Consider this an exercise from Mr. Lowe. He wants to see how much you can figure out on your own."

Despite the Analyst's words, Intuition's instincts told her the Southern Knights situation wouldn't be the subject of her evening briefing. True to her new title, she paid close attention to her instincts and concentrated on other tasks and questions. Promptly at 6:00 PM, after the analysts left for the day, the Analyst led her through No Man's Land to the Door. "Your biometrics are in the system now. Please test them."

Intuition put her right hand on the biometric reader next to the Door and looked into the retina scanner. The Door slid open, and they entered the elevator. She repeated the process with the biometric reader inside the elevator. Its door slid shut, and the elevator descended.

During the descent, the Analyst took her hand. "As I'm certain you noticed yesterday, Mr. Lowe doesn't use titles in our meetings. I'm Wes, not the Analyst, and you're Gayle, not Intuition."

"I noticed, but appreciate the clarification."

Half-a-minute later, the door opened on Mr. Lowe's suite.

Unlike her first visit, when her mind still reeled from the unexpected turn of events, Gayle was ready for this visit. Her gaze flicked around the sitting room, and her mind recorded minor details. She let her analytical training loose on her observations. But, as befitted her new title, she gave her intuition free rein, too. And the answer proved both logical and intuitive. So much so that she gave a microscopic nod.

Mr. Lowe noticed her nod. "I believe Gayle has figured it out."

"I believe she has, sir," Wes said.

"How long did it take you to reach the same conclusion, Wes?"

"Four weeks and six days after my father first introduced me to you."

Gayle's eyes widened. "Your father?"

Wes nodded. "He was Mr. Lowe's previous Analyst."

"Wes's father was an excellent Analyst, as were his grandfather, great grandfather, and a dozen more of his ancestors," Mr. Lowe said. "But Wes has surpassed them all."

Another piece of the puzzle that was Mr. Lowe clicked into place in Gayle's mind. Her second conclusion pleased Gayle so thoroughly, she couldn't keep the pleasure out of her expression.

Again, Mr. Lowe noticed, and he gave a delighted laugh. "I believe Gayle has realized something else, Wes. A conclusion that still eludes you, if I'm not mistaken."

Wes's brows drew down in concentration. "What have I missed, sir?"

Mr. Lowe waved to a loveseat across from his chair. "We'll get to it soon, my boy. Take a seat, both of you." After they sat, Mr. Lowe looked at Gayle. "Why don't you tell us what you noticed when you entered the room, and what conclusions you drew?"

Gayle took a deep breath. "The easiest observation is this loveseat, which wasn't here yesterday. But that mostly ties into my second conclusion."

"Mostly?" Mr. Lowe asked.

"The faux leather upholstery contributed to my first conclusion. As did the spacing between your seat and this one. The low table helps hide it, but your chair is at least twice as far from ours than is normal in such an intimate setting. The laminate floor covering is another tip off. I don't know your net worth, but you casually sacrificed thirty-six mechs worth hundreds of billions of dollars yesterday. The difference between this upholstery and flooring and the best that money can buy is less than a rounding error to you. So there must be a reason you selected such cheap materials."

Gayle pointed at the table next to Mr. Lowe's chair. "The atomizer on the side table is another clue. As are both your incredible age and your second most pressing question." Mr. Lowe raised his eyebrows. Gayle took it as an invitation to continue, and said, "You want to know why you're still alive after twenty-two hundred years."

"How does that question tie into your conclusion?" Mr. Lowe asked.

"You don't know *why* you're still alive, which means you also don't know *what* might cause your death. Life is precious to all humans, but I imagine it's even more so to someone your age."

"And you got all of that from the way I furnished this room?"

Gayle shrugged. "Faux leather and laminate are easily disinfected. I believe the atomizer contains an airborne disinfectant."

She pointed at one of two doors in the room. "That door has an airtight seal. At a guess, there's a decontamination chamber beyond it, which keeps germs from getting into your living quarters." Gayle pointed at a second door. "That's a normal door. I assume it leads to a standard set of living quarters, perhaps for use if you wish female companionship? After they go through a thorough decontamination process, of course."

"You are correct on all accounts," Mr. Lowe said. "And your second conclusion?"

Gayle leaned against Wes. "You sent Wes and me on the date last night because you want us to get married."

"What?" Wes cried. "Why?"

"In part, because Mr. Lowe wants you to be happy," Gayle said.

"Only in part?" Wes asked.

"Yes." Gayle looked at Mr. Lowe. "There are thirteen female analysts besides me. We're all two to five years younger than Wes. You hired us in the hopes one of us would catch Wes's eye, didn't you?"

"I did," Mr. Lowe said.

"Sir," Wes said, "you hired women with the expectation I'd find one of them sexually appealing?"

Mr. Lowe nodded. "I had hoped you'd find a woman on your own. But you obviously needed a push, so I surrounded you with young, attractive, intelligent women. And it worked."

"But... why, sir?"

"That's the other part." Gayle turned Wes's face towards her and gave him a soft kiss on the lips. "The next Analyst isn't going to conceive himself, you know."

"My dear, I've had high hopes for you since I observed your initial interview." Mr. Lowe clapped his hands in delight. "But you have far exceeded this old man's wildest dreams!"

"You *planned* all of this, sir?" Wes asked.

Gayle shook her head. "Mr. Lowe set the stage, Wes. And he shoved me into your path. Then he just waited for nature to take its course. It's taken seven years, but..." Gayle ducked her head and her lips curved up in a demure smile. "Nature *is* going to take its course, isn't it?"

Wes stammered, "I... That is... Um..." Then an answering smile lit Wes's face. "Yes. Yes, it is."

Gayle reached up and tapped Wes's nose with a finger. "Then don't you have a question to pop?"

To Gayle's pleasure, Wes slid off the loveseat and knelt before her. "Gayle, will you marry me?"

Gayle tilted her head up and tapped her chin. "Let me think..." She leaned forward and kissed Wes. "Yes, I'll marry you."

Wes stood and pulled Gayle up from the loveseat. "Sir, we need the Ferrari and the penthouse again."

Mr. Lowe nodded his assent and waved them towards the elevator. "Pick up an engagement ring while you're in town. Buy whatever Gayle wants, regardless of cost."

Simple observation told Gayle that Mr. Lowe expected a reaction, so she gasped and clapped her hands in delight. "You're too generous, sir!"

Mr. Lowe smiled at her objections. "Nonsense. As you said mere moments ago, the expense is less than a rounding error to me."

Guided by her intuition, Gayle bit her lip and furrowed her brow. "If only..." She gave her head a shake and turned towards the elevator. "No."

Mr. Lowe smiled. "If only what, my dear?"

"It's silly, sir. And impossible."

"Let me be the judge of that."

Gayle looked down, as if unwilling to meet Mr. Lowe's gaze.

"I have an overwhelming desire to hug you, sir. But I haven't been thoroughly decontaminated."

Mr. Lowe stood up and opened his arms. "I'm sure I'll survive a single hug, Gayle. Perhaps even a kiss on the cheek."

Gayle hurried to Mr. Lowe, pulled him into a tight hug, and gave him a quick peck on the cheek. She disentangled herself, let her cheeks redden, and backed away. "Thank you, sir."

"By the ages, Wes," Mr. Lowe said, "I envy you!" He shooed them towards the elevator. "Now go have a fun night, you two."

As they stepped into the elevator, Gayle looked back at Mr. Lowe. "I know I'm not supposed to talk business tonight, but I must warn you that your plan to convince the Southern Knights to leave Atlanta won't work."

Mr. Lowe frowned. "Why not?"

"I will explain now, if you wish," Gayle said. "Wes and I can postpone our evening out if—"

"No, you kids go have fun. When you're as old as I am, waiting a few hours is easy." His face assumed a thoughtful expression. "Maybe it'll give me time to figure out why you believe that."

As the elevator door slid shut, Gayle melted into Wes's embrace and kissed him. The question forming on his lips vanished, and he returned her kiss.

After the kiss, Gayle leaned her head on Wes's shoulder and sighed in contentment. *My mother was right. No matter their age or station in life, men are simple creatures. And so easy to manipulate.*

THIS HAS GONE FAR ENOUGH

Bryan cooked breakfast, as he had done the previous morning. But all five Knights were already gathered around the kitchen table as he worked. David's fingers tapped on a tablet computer while the others got settled.

"Did anyone else have trouble sleeping last night?" Kristin asked.

"Yes." Connie massaged her forehead. "And even when I fell asleep, I had nightmares where Mickey Mouse and Donald Duck had a shootout with the Vegas team over us."

"That is good to hear," Aramis suddenly realized how his comment must have sounded. "Please do not believe I am happy that you suffered nightmares, Connie!"

"I know." Connie patted Aramis's arm. "I'm guessing you had nightmares, too?"

The young sorcerer nodded. "I dreamt of a large mouse that resembled the clown who visited yesterday. He had long, sharp teeth and claws, and chased me through this house. I could not concentrate well enough to weave spells against the demon mouse. Fortunately, I awoke just as the mouse opened its mouth to bite me."

David suddenly drew back from the tablet's screen. "What the hell?"

"Is that an exclamation of surprise or alarm?" Mark asked.

"Yes."

Kristin spoke around a huge yawn. "You've lost us, bossman."

David looked up from the tablet. "According to this news story, we're moving to San Diego."

Mark's eyebrows rose. "They didn't even send a team with a proposal."

"I know." David shook his head. "It doesn't make any sense."

"That, um..." Bryan hesitated, then rushed on. "That's my fault, David."

"How?"

"After all the proposal groups left yesterday, I tried to get some work done in the yard. To repair the damage those people made, tromping all over the garden, and to relax after that circus."

"It was definitely a circus," Mark agreed.

"Yeah," Kristin muttered. "And that's the only thing Tina Horne got right in her stupid news report last night."

"Anyway," Bryan continued, "that's when all the reporters showed up. I kept the front gate closed, so they didn't get in. But they stood at the gate and yelled questions at me about the proposals. Especially which city you guys favored. They didn't believe me when I told them I didn't know anything." Bryan shrugged. "I finally got tired of it, and just blurted out the first city name that came to mind."

"San Diego," David said.

"Yeah. Sorry for doing something so stupid."

"Don't worry about it," Kristin said. "I'll bet you showed more patience than I would have. *My* solution would have involved dragging reporters back to their cars and stuffing them inside."

Bryan smiled. "I'd have paid good money to see something like that!"

The telephone rang, and David rose to answer the phone. "Hello... Yes, you've reached the Southern Knights."

"Anyone want to bet that's Barl calling to tell us goodbye, and good riddance?" Kristin asked. Another thought crossed her mind, and Kristin grinned. "No, even better. I bet it's the mayor of San Diego calling about that news story!"

"No, Mr. Mayor," David said, "you didn't call too early."

"No way," Kristin said. "It can't be."

"Thank you, but the news story is erroneous," David said. After a few seconds, he added, "I'm sure San Diego is a lovely city for crime fighting, but we're happy right here in Atlanta." He listened for a moment, then gave a polite laugh. "I agree, sir. The Southern California Knights just doesn't flow off the tongue. Thank you for understanding."

After David hung up the phone, he just stared at it for a long moment. He lifted the handset again. "This has gone too far."

As David tapped buttons, Connie asked, "Who are you calling, David?"

"City hall. It's time to put an end to all of this."

Electrode and Dragon landed on the sidewalk before city hall, and Dragon's three passengers descended from his back. Dragon concentrated, and his twenty-ton bulk shrank to a two hundred pound man.

Electrode glanced at his team. "Is everyone ready?"

"Yes," Connie said.

"I am," Aramis said.

"I'm as ready as I'll ever be." Kristin headed for the entrance. "Let's get this over with."

Mark simply nodded and fell in beside Kristin.

Five minutes later, a secretary showed the Southern Knights into the city council meeting chambers. The full council, presided over by the mayor and backed by a dozen aides, sat behind a U-shaped table, and watched with stony silence as the Knights filed in.

"I am most disappointed," the mayor said without preamble. "Most disappointed, indeed, that you have seen fit to entertain proposals from other cities, without even giving Atlanta the opportunity to make a counteroffer." The mayor's face assumed a grave expression as he shook his head. "To think that you would even *consider* moving your franchise—"

An aide bent over and whispered in the mayor's ear. The mayor gave a quick nod and waved the aide away. "To think that you would even *consider* moving your superhero team to another city wounds me. The Southern Knights were born here. They grew to national prominence here. And I speak for all Atlantans when I say the Southern Knights should *stay* here!"

"That's why we're here, sir," Electrode said. "To clear up a misunderstanding."

"Didn't like the offers you got yesterday?" a woman to the mayor's left sneered.

"The proposals we received yesterday were all quite generous," Electrode said.

The woman sniffed. "So now you're here to find out how much you can get from *our* city coffers?"

Electrode began, "Our sole aim is—"

"To extort as much money from the city of Atlanta as you can," the woman snapped.

That proved too much for Kristin. She stalked towards the

woman, her eyes blazing. "Are you Tina Horne's sister or something?"

Alarm crossed the council member's face, and she pushed her chair back from the table. "Wha-? Why?"

Kristin put her hands on the table and leaned towards the councilwoman. "Because I can only think of two reasons to repeat Horne's idiotic talking points. Either you're related to her, or you're stupid." Kristin stared into the woman's eye. "You don't *look* stupid, so—"

"You're not helping, Kristin," Electrode said.

"Yeah, I know." Kristin turned and walked back to join her friends. "It's just this whole situation is really getting on my nerves."

"I must say," the mayor said, "this display is an insult to this council."

Tiny lightning bolts arced in Electrode's hair as he regarded the mayor. "So is your insistence that we came here to extort money from the city." He folded his arms and swept his glowing eyes over the council. "Especially since we came to tell you that we have no intention of moving. Atlanta is our city, and we enjoy serving its citizens."

The mayor considered Electrode's words. "But you must want something in return, Electrode."

"I do, Mr. Mayor." Electrode sighed. "I want you and the council to join us for a press conference, where we'll announce that we're not moving."

"And that we never even considered moving," Kristin added.

Electrode nodded his agreement with Kristin's addition.

"That's all?" the mayor asked.

"That's all."

"Well, that's, um, reasonable." The mayor turned to the aide standing behind him. "Call a news conference for..." He looked back at Electrode. "Is 4:00 PM acceptable?"

"It is."

The mayor turned back to the aide. "News conference at 4:00 PM in the city hall press room."

"And make sure Tina Horne is there," Kristin growled. "Maybe she can get the story straight this time."

Tina Horne arrived two hours before the news conference, assuring herself a front and center seat. Her cameraman, Bob, settled into the seat next to her and began checking his equipment.

"What do you think this is about?" Bob asked.

Even though she'd just walked through the empty room, Tina glanced over her shoulder to make sure no one was eavesdropping. "An announcement that the Southern Knights are staying in Atlanta, along with some claptrap about how they never planned on leaving."

"So, your basic photo op for the politicians?"

"With cliché platitudes from the Knights, about how they love Atlanta and wouldn't dream of leaving."

"What *won't* they mention?" Bob asked.

"All the off the books perks the city offered the Southern Knights." Tina counted items off on her fingers. "Tax breaks. Grants from 'private' charitable organizations that exist to funnel city funds to anyone the politicians favor. Guarantees that city officials will defend anything the Knights do. You know, the usual."

"What do you need me to do?"

Tina flashed a predatory smile at Bob. "Keep filming, no matter what."

Promptly at 4:00 PM, Atlanta's mayor, city council, and the Southern Knights entered the packed press room. Connie's eyes swept the room and fought against her natural inclination to turn around and leave the stage. Her face remained impassive, belying the turmoil inside her head.

You fight criminals and villains all the time, she thought. *Often in front of far larger crowds and just as many cameras. Why is this so much harder?* But Connie knew the answer. *When I'm in action, the crowds and cameras are incidental to the event. Here, they* are *the event.*

Kristin leaned towards Connie and whispered, "Look who's sitting right up front. How much do you want to bet she's been sitting there for hours, just waiting to hit us with stupid questions?"

With the soft whir of Bob's camera coming from beside her, Tina caught Kristin's eye and offered a frosty smile.

Connie whispered, "Be careful, Kristin. Her cameraman is filming."

"I know." Kristin returned Tina's smile with a broad grin and waved. "Hi Tina! I see you got my invitation."

Tina's brows drew down in confusion. Then her eyes hardened and she opened her mouth to reply. But the mayor spoke first.

"Hello everyone." He turned his attention to the Southern Knights. "I'm sure you're all wondering why I've called you here."

The gathered members of the press laughed politely. All except Tina Horne.

As the laughter died away, she called, "We're not wondering why we're here, Mr. Mayor. We're wondering what excuses you'll give for knuckling under to the Southern Knights' extortion."

The mayor glared at Tina. "Now see here—"

"Spare us your protestations," Tina said. "Everyone knows

you want to maintain the supposed prestige Atlanta gets from having the Southern Knights based here."

"Ms. Horne—"

"What we *don't* know is how much you're willing to take from the city coffers to keep them here." Tina raised her voice to be heard over the protestations from the mayor and the council members. "We're sure your financial people know many devious ways to hide the payments. We're equally sure we'll find round-about payments to the Knights, if we dig deeply enough into the city's finances."

With her eyes blazing, Kristin balled her fists and took a step towards Tina. But Connie caught her friend's arm. "Don't, Kristin."

"But it's all lies!" Kristin said.

"I know, but it's aimed at you, not the city officials. Her cameraman has been filming you exclusively, from the beginning."

Kristin looked at Connie. "I don't care. I can't let her get away with those insinuations."

"I agree," Connie said. "But let me handle this."

Kristin stared into Connie's eyes, then nodded.

Tina's cameraman shifted his focus to Connie when she broke away from her friends and strode towards Tina. He zoomed in on her calm demeanor and dispassionate eyes, shuddered, and zoomed out again.

Silence fell across the room as Connie stopped in front of Tina. The reporter tried to take the initiative, as she had with the mayor. "I can't believe you're the team spokesperson. You never talk to the press, except to offer the blandest—"

"Be quiet." Connie didn't raise her voice, but her words cut through Tina's tirade.

"Excuse me?" Tina snapped. "Just who do you think—"

"I said, be quiet." Again, Connie's tone never changed.

The barest quaver entered Tina's voice. "O- or... what?"

"I will be displeased."

Tina rallied. "Ooooo. How terrifying!"

Bob found Connie's tone alarming and offered a warning. "Tina, I think—"

Tina glared at him. "You're paid to film, not think."

Bob kept filming.

"You should listen to him," Connie said.

"Why?" Tina snapped. "Seriously, Ms. Ronnin, what are you going to do if I don't?"

"I don't know yet." Connie leaned towards Tina until their faces were two inches apart. Then she whispered, "But I promise you won't enjoy it."

Tina turned her head wildly, catching the eye of every reporter she could. "She threatened me! You all heard it!"

"You threatened and insulted my friends," Connie said. "Why is your behavior acceptable while mine is not?" Connie turned to the mayor. "Mr. Mayor, I believe this press conference will go smoother without the presence of Ms. Horne."

The mayor nodded. "I agree. Ms. Horne, remove yourself from my press room."

Connie turned her disquieting gaze on Bob. "Did you get that?"

"Every word," he said. "Every gesture."

"Good. I suggest your station show it. In its entirety."

Bob swallowed. "I'll, um, relay your suggestion to the station manager."

Connie returned to her friends as Tina and Bob skulked from the press room.

Kristin met her with a wide grin. "Damn, girl, that was badass!"

As Connie suggested, the press conference went smoother without Tina.

EXPENDABLE

Gayle, Wes, and Mr. Lowe sat in their usual seats, with Wes's laptop on the table between them. The Southern Knights' press conference filled the screen. A well-dressed man in late middle-age, with a microphone gripped in his right hand, stood to address the Knights.

"You've told us you asked nothing from the city except this press conference," he said. He flashed the inquisitive smile that made him one of the most popular reporters in Atlanta. "Most of the delegations who visited you yesterday revealed the offers they presented, and even the least of them was… generous."

The reporter paused, obviously waiting for one of the Knights to respond. Electrode didn't play along. "That's correct."

The reporter laughed. "You're going to make me ask the question, aren't you?"

Electrode grinned. "Got it in one, Carl."

Carl gave a rueful shake of his head. "Very well, Electrode, *why* didn't you accept one of those lucrative offers?"

"May I take this one?" Kristin asked.

Electrode gestured for her to go ahead. Carl nodded his assent at the same time.

Gayle voiced the answer at the same time Kristin did. "Because Atlanta is our home."

Wes and Mr. Lowe both stared at Gayle. As Wes closed his laptop, he said, "That was a live broadcast."

"I know," Gayle said.

"But you knew what Kristin was going to say, word for word."

"Before she said it," Mr. Lowe added.

Gayle's lips turned up at the corners. "I did."

"When did you figure it out?" Wes asked.

"Yesterday morning. About a minute after I figured out why Mr. Lowe ran that expensive test of superhero teams around the world."

Wes frowned. "I didn't tell you Mr. Lowe's reasoning."

"I wouldn't be much of an intuitive analyst if I couldn't figure that out."

Mr. Lowe cleared his throat. "If you've figured it out, please enlighten us. Why did I test the world's top superhero teams?"

"You want to find the best team, lure them to Denver, and then shower them with sizable philanthropic contributions to their cause."

"Why would I do such a thing?" Mr. Lowe asked.

"To engender loyalty to you," Gayle said. "Should so-called supervillains or mercenaries hired by a rival attack this facility, you could count on the loyal superheroes rushing to your aide."

"But hardly anyone knows I exist," Mr. Lowe said, "and they all work for me."

"Not even you believe that, sir."

Mr. Lowe raised an eyebrow. "Why do you say that?"

"There's only one way to keep a secret in this digital age. You must live alone on a desert island, and never have anything to do with people. *Any* people." Gayle leaned back in the loveseat.

"You know the old saying—two can keep a secret if one of them is dead."

Mr. Lowe glanced around the room. "My desert island has a mountain on top of it, but otherwise..."

Gayle shook her head. "At least a hundred of your employees know you exist. Also, no matter how cautious your accountants are and how many shell corporations exist between you and your holdings, your financial dealings leave an enormous digital footprint." Gayle shook her head. "As much as you might wish otherwise, some people know you exist, including several with close ties to the Southern Knights."

"Such as?"

Gayle shrugged. "Dragon's mate, Serpent, and her partners, Synergy, almost certainly. And if they know... Well, they *are* information brokers. Then there are the remnants of Serpent's old organization, Viper. Even in its reduced state, its reach goes wide and deep." Gayle met Mr. Lowe's gaze. "And those are the ones I thought of without performing any research."

"Which makes my desire to bring the Southern Knights to Denver all the more pressing," Mr. Lowe said.

Gayle shook her head. "Denver's delegation can follow all of the social conventions, something made easier by the way the other delegations acted yesterday. They can make the most lucrative offer. But they won't convince the Knights to leave Atlanta. And no amount of pressure from Tina Horne will change their minds."

"Then what do you think I should do?"

"You could move to Atlanta. I'm sure the Knights would welcome philanthropic investments in their cause, provided you could assure them you wouldn't turn out like Jonathan Barl."

Mr. Lowe shook his head. "I selected this location for many reasons, including the medical and military advantages its isolation provides. I'm not moving."

Gayle's eyes unfocused. "Have you considered making an offer to one of the eleven superhero teams who lost to the mechs you sent against them? They're all unpopular in their home cities, right now. I'm certain one of them will leap at the opportunity for a fresh start in a new city."

Again, Mr. Lowe shook his head. "I want the best. Period."

"May I assume you heard the finality in Kristin's voice? Luring the Knights from Atlanta will take considerably more leverage than that Horne woman can fabricate."

"I have a fallback plan," Mr. Lowe said.

"Sir, we've discussed this," Wes said. "It won't work."

"What won't work?" Gayle asked.

"A plan guaranteed to give me leverage over the Southern Knights," Mr. Lowe said.

Gayle looked back and forth between Wes and Mr. Lowe, but they stayed silent. She sighed. "I'm intuitive, not a mind reader."

Wes looked at the wall behind Mr. Lowe. "He wants to kidnap Serpent's and Dragon's hatchling."

Gayle turned wide eyes on Mr. Lowe. "You want to kidnap the only dragon hatchling in the world?"

Mr. Lowe's gaze turned icy. "It will give me leverage."

Gayle shook her head. "You will die if you try that."

"That's what I told him," Wes said.

With a petulance out of character for a twenty-two hundred-year-old man, Mr. Lowe said, "I think we could make it work."

In unison, Wes and Gayle said, "No, we can't."

"But," Gayle added, "it could be the first step in a plan that could work. Maybe…"

The two men turned surprised looks on Gayle. Mr. Lowe said, "Explain."

"Fear is a poor motivator," Gayle said. "But gratitude? That could be a game changer."

"Impossible," Mr. Lowe snorted. "No parent will thank me for abducting their child."

"Of course not," she said. "But they will thank you for *rescuing* their child from the criminals who took him."

"Criminals *I* will hire to perform the job. You just told me my finances aren't as covert as I wish. What's to stop Serpent and Synergy from tracking the payments back to me?"

"You have several caches of gold, don't you? None of which are listed with a financial institution?"

"Yes, but—"

"Among the many employees who work for you, both directly and indirectly, I know of nine who are just clever enough to embezzle from you. But they're not so clever they remained undetected." Gayle caught and held Mr. Lowe's gaze. "If you're willing to sacrifice one of them, I have an idea that might achieve your ends."

Interest flashed in Mr. Lowe's eyes. "Except for Wes and you, *all* of my employees are expendable."

"Then we just have to select the right embezzler, suborn him into performing the negotiations with a capable but financially strapped mercenary group, and let the embezzler pay them with your untraceable gold." Gayle flashed a tight smile. "Do I need to explain further?"

Mr. Lowe returned her smile. "No, my dear, you don't."

Wes leaned over and kissed her on the top of her head. "Good work, Intuition."

Gayle let her cheeks color. *It is good, isn't it, Wes? It's a pity you'll never know* how *good it is. Every girl must have her secrets. But mine will rid us of this old fossil. And then* we *will rule his empire together.*

ABOUT THE AUTHOR

Henry Vogel began his writing career in comic books way back in the 1980s, with the indie titles *Southern Knights* and *X-Thieves*. When the bottom dropped out of the black & white comic book market, Henry went into IT, where he worked for the next thirty-three years. Henry took up professional storytelling in 2006, and has performed all across his home state of North Carolina.

As a lifetime fan of science fiction, Henry always wanted to write science fiction novels. He began writing *Scout's Honor* in 2012, and released it to the world in 2014. He hasn't stopped writing since.

Henry makes his home in Raleigh, NC, and is hard at work on his next novel.

www.henryvogelwrites.com

ALSO BY HENRY VOGEL

Travis & Trouble

Trouble in Twi-Town

Trouble on Mars

The Fortune Chronicles

Fortune's Fool

The Scales of Sin & Sorrow

The Scout Series

Scout's Honor

Scout's Oath

Scout's Duty

Scout's Law

Scout's Training

Scout's First Mission

Hart for Adventure

The Princess Scout

Scout: The Lost Colony Adventures

Non-series books

The Lost Planet

Heart of Dorkness & Other Stories

The Connaught Family Chronicles

The Fugitive Heir

The Fugitive Pair

The Fugitive Snare

The Hostage in Hiding

The Captain Nancy Martin

The Counterfeit Captain

The Undercover Captain

The Recognition Series

The Recognition Run

The Recognition Rejection

The Recognition Revelation

Comic Books

Aristocratic Xraterrestrial Time-Traveling Thieves Complete Collection

Southern Knights Almost Complete Collection

Southern Knights Color Edition

Southern Knights: The Morrigan Wars

Southern Knights: Leaving Atlanta (prose novella)

Missing Beings

Illustrated Children's Book

I'm in Charge! and Other Stories